CATS AT THE CAMPGROUND

"Before you do anything, I think there's something else you should see . . ." said Wilfred Bennett.

Exchanging surprised glances, Mandy and James followed the old man into his backyard. What was he going to show them?

Wilfred led them across the yard to where a narrow passageway ran between the cottage and the campsite fence. "There," he said.

Mandy stepped forward. The passageway was half covered by the overhanging roof of the cottage and at the far end it was shadowy and dimly lit. She could just make out a pile of old newspapers and there in the newspapers were . . .

"Kittens!" she gasped.

Give someone you love a home!
Read about the animals of Animal Ark™

CATS at the CAMPGROUND

Ben M. Baglio

Illustrations by Ann Baum

Cover illustration by
Mary Ann Lasher

AN
APPLE
PAPERBACK

SCHOLASTIC INC.

New York Toronto London Auckland Sydney
Mexico City New Delhi Hong Kong Buenos Aires

**Special thanks to Linda Chapman.
Thanks also to C. J. Hall,
B.Vet.Med., M.R.C.V.S., for reviewing
the veterinary information contained in this book.**

ISBN 0-439-34393-3

12 11 10 9 8 7 6 5 4 3 2 1   2 3 4 5 6 7/0

Printed in the U.S.A.   40
First Scholastic printing, May 2002

TM

One

Mandy Hope gazed down at Dylan, the sick puppy who had been brought into Animal Ark the day before. "You're being such a brave boy," she said softly, stroking the puppy's head.

The young Bernese mountain dog, who was recovering from an operation on his spine, looked up at Mandy with soulful brown eyes. He was only four months old and still had his fluffy puppy coat. Mandy smoothed his silky black ears and lightly touched each of his sweet tan eyebrows.

Just then, the door opened. Dr. Emily Hope, Mandy's mother, came in. "How is he?" she asked quietly. Her long red hair was tied back but, as usual, soft strands were escaping around her face.

"He's still not moving," Mandy replied, her blue eyes full of worry. "He *is* going to get better, isn't he, Mom?"

Dr. Emily leaned into Dylan's cage and gently examined the row of stitches that ran down the back of the pup's neck. "I hope so, love. I really do," she replied. "But it's going to be a few days before your dad and I know whether the operation has been a success."

"What would have happened if you hadn't operated?" Mandy asked, looking at the doleful puppy.

"His condition would have deteriorated quickly," her mom explained. "He had a cyst — a swelling — growing in his spine. It was stopping his muscles from getting the right messages from his brain. If we hadn't operated, then it would have gotten bigger, eventually paralyzing him." She stroked the puppy gently as she spoke. "It was a complicated operation, but if we hadn't done it, then Dylan would have had to be put to sleep. At least, this way, we've given him a chance."

Mandy nodded, feeling a little better.

"Let's leave him to rest, love," Dr. Emily said. "There's nothing more we can do now."

Giving Dylan a kiss on his head, Mandy shut the cage door. She followed her mom out of the residential unit where all the Animal Ark patients that were too ill to go home were kept. Animal Ark, an old stone cottage with a modern red-brick extension, was both Mandy's home and her parents' veterinary clinic.

"Now, didn't you say something about visiting Wilfred Bennett and Matty this morning?" Dr. Emily said as they went into the cozy, oak-beamed kitchen.

"Yes," said Mandy, taking off the white coat she always wore when she was helping with the patients. She cheered up slightly as she thought of her plans for the first day of spring break. "I'm meeting James at the Fox and Goose crossroads at ten o'clock, and then we're going on to Wilfred's house." Wilfred Bennett had once run the local riding school. A short while ago, his wife, Rose, had died and Wilfred had been forced to close the school. He had sold all of the horses, apart from Rose's gray mare, Matty, who was Mandy's favorite.

"Well, give Matty a hug from me," Dr. Emily said.

"And an apple?" said Mandy, looking hopefully at the large fruit bowl on the kitchen table.

Her mom smiled. "And an apple," she said.

"Thanks, Mom," Mandy said, pulling on a jacket and stuffing the biggest apple into her pocket.

Dr. Emily glanced at her watch. "Did you just say you were meeting James at ten?"

Mandy nodded.

Her mother raised her eyebrows. "Well, you'd better get a move on. It's five minutes past already."

"Oh, no!" Mandy gasped. She had been so busy with Dylan that she had completely lost track of time. "James'll be mad!"

"Bye!" Dr. Emily laughed, as Mandy grabbed her scarf and ran out of the door.

It only took Mandy a few seconds to jump onto her bike. She pedaled furiously past the wooden sign that read ANIMAL ARK VETERINARY CLINIC and down the lane that led to the main road. A biting February wind blew Mandy's short, dark-blond hair back from her face, but she was cycling so hard that she hardly felt the cold.

As she got near the crossroads, she saw James Hunter, her best friend, and Blackie, his Labrador, waiting by the signpost. James was standing by his bike, his glasses halfway down his nose as usual.

"What time do you call this?" he said, pretending to be indignant, as Mandy braked beside him.

"Sorry," she panted, her cheeks flushed from the wind and exercise. She patted Blackie, who was leaping around her ecstatically. "I was with Dylan."

"Oh, how is he?" James asked quickly. Mandy had called him up the night before to tell him all about the puppy's operation.

"Still not moving," Mandy replied. Blackie jumped up at her, almost sending her and her bike flying. "Blackie!" she said sternly. "Down!"

Blackie backed off. Mandy quickly stroked him to show that she didn't mean to be cross with him. She had known Blackie ever since he had been a tiny puppy and she adored him. As she scratched his ears, he thumped his tail against the ground. "He's frisky today," she said to James.

"He hasn't been for a walk yet," James said. He looked rather sheepish. "Actually, I overslept — I only got here about a minute ago."

"And you let *me* feel guilty!" Mandy exclaimed, reaching out to punch his arm.

James dodged and grinned. "I couldn't resist it! Come on, let's go. If we cycle fast, it might tire Blackie out."

They biked along the hilly road that led out of Welford village, with Blackie bounding happily beside them. The tree branches were still bare but along the roadside there were clumps of nodding white snowdrops and the first early daffodils could just be seen pushing their green tips out of the ground.

Wilfred Bennett's small stone cottage stood by the roadside just outside the village. The rolling land behind it, which had once been Wilfred's riding school, was now fenced off and a sign by the entrance leading into it read ROSE OF YORKSHIRE CAMPSITE.

"I wonder when the campsite will be opening again for the summer," Mandy said to James as they leaned their bikes against the fence.

"Maybe Wilfred will know," James said. He called Blackie, who was sniffing in some long grass. Blackie trotted over and sat obediently to have his leash clipped onto his collar. "There, you're not naughty all the time, are you?" James said, glancing at Mandy.

She grinned. "Just most of it!"

They went to Wildred's front door and banged the horse-shaped brass knocker. A few moments later, the door opened and Wilfred Bennett's kind old face peered out.

"Hi, Wilfred," Mandy said. "We've come to visit."

Wilfred's weather-beaten cheeks creased even more as he smiled broadly. "Well, that's what I call a coincidence," he said in his deep Yorkshire accent. "I was going to give you two a call this morning. I've got a little problem and I thought you might be able to help."

"What is it?" James asked curiously.

But before Wilfred could reply, a thin gray cat came trotting around the corner of the cottage. Mandy looked at it in surprise. Wilfred didn't have a cat.

Suddenly, Blackie spotted the cat, too. With an excited bark, he lunged forward, almost pulling James off his feet.

The cat froze for half a second and then, like lightning, it streaked across the road and vanished under the far hedge in a blur of dark gray fur.

"Blackie!" James cried. "How many times have I told you not to do that?"

Blackie sat down again, looking contrite. But Mandy grinned as she noticed a slight wag in the Labrador's tail. She turned to Wilfred. "Whose cat is that?" she asked. "I haven't seen it before."

"I don't rightly know," Wilfred replied. "But it's my guess she was one of Arthur Oldfield's cats."

"Oh! Poor thing!" Mandy gasped. She had heard her parents talking about Arthur Oldfield a while ago. He had been a bit of a recluse, his only company being the handful of pedigree British Blue cats he kept. But last summer he died, and his distraught pets had run off and begun to live wild.

Wilfred nodded gravely. "I've seen several gray cats like his around here," he added. "That one turned up yesterday and made a home in my backyard." He rubbed his chin. "I put a little food out for her," he said. "But the problem is, I'm allergic to cats, so I'd like it if she found another home. That's why I was going to call you. I thought you might be able to help," he explained.

"Of course we will," Mandy said immediately. She and James had often rescued stray animals before —

dogs, cats, and all sorts of wildlife. But her parents had a strict rule about taking in stray animals at Animal Ark. "We have enough animal responsibilities as it is," her mom always said. However, Mandy was sure that kind-hearted Betty Hilder, who ran the nearby animal sanctuary, would be happy to take the cat.

Already Mandy's mind was whirling, but before she could say anything else, Wilfred spoke again. "Before you do anything, I think there's something else you should see . . ." he said.

Exchanging surprised glances, Mandy and James followed Wilfred into his backyard. What was he going to show them?

Wilfred's backyard was tiny, only little more than a square of concrete containing a trash can and a coal bin. He led them across the yard to where a narrow passageway ran between the cottage and the campsite fence. He nodded at the passageway. "There," he said.

Mandy stepped forward. The passageway was half covered by the overhanging roof of the cottage and at the far end it was shadowy and dimly lit. She could just make out a pile of old newspapers and there in the newspapers were . . .

"Kittens!" she gasped.

Huddled together in a makeshift newspaper nest were three small kittens. Two were gray and white and one was black with a white triangle on its chest. They crouched together, their eyes blinking. From the size of them, Mandy guessed they must be three to four weeks old. She swung around. "Are they the gray cat's?"

"Yes," Wilfred said, nodding. "She brought them here yesterday. It's my guess she was looking for somewhere safe for them, but they can't stay here — it's too cold. They need to be inside."

Blackie pulled on his leash, whining in his eagerness to go and investigate the kittens. They shrank back nervously against the paper, making tiny meowing sounds.

"I'd better keep Blackie away from them," James said quickly. "He might scare them."

Mandy nodded. "I'll see how friendly they are," she said. She edged cautiously into the narrow passageway. The kittens drew back a little. Careful not to alarm them, Mandy crouched down and crawled slowly on her knees toward them. The ground was damp but Mandy didn't care. Her eyes were fixed on the three kittens.

As she drew closer, she could see their markings more clearly. Both gray-and-white kittens had gray heads and white chests, but one was smaller than the other and had a white smudge on its muzzle and white front legs. The third kitten was jet-black apart from the white triangle on its chest and four white paws. They stared at her, their eyes huge in their skinny faces, their pointed ears standing upright.

"Here, little ones," Mandy murmured, stopping and holding out her hand. "I'm not going to hurt you."

The black kitten ventured forward a few steps; he was still so young that his movements were uncoordinated and his legs unsteady.

Mandy stayed still and waited. "Come on," she coaxed softly. "It's OK."

The black kitten wobbled closer. Very slowly, Mandy reached out and tickled him under his chin. He opened his mouth and meowed loudly.

Mandy smiled. He was absolutely adorable. Hearing his meow, the other two kittens began to come toward her. They were too young to have any real fear of humans and soon they were crowding around her as she stroked and tickled them. The little female was shivering slightly and all three of them felt cold.

"They seem very friendly," James said from the entrance to the passageway.

Mandy looked around. "They are." Reluctantly, she placed them back in their nest and backed out. "But we've got to get them somewhere warm and dry." She stroked Blackie, who was sniffing eagerly at the kitten smell on her jeans.

"Here's the mother," Wilfred said softly, nodding at the yard entrance.

James immediately tightened his hold on Blackie's leash. Seeing them, the mother cat stopped in her tracks.

"It's all right," Mandy said, crouching down. "We won't hurt you."

But the cat didn't seem to believe her. Turning on the spot, she fled back through the gate.

"Why's she so frightened?" James said, looking puzzled. "I mean, she must have been tame when she belonged to Mr. Oldfield."

Wilfred rubbed his chin thoughtfully. "Well, I'd say that judging by the size of her, she can't have been much more than a kitten when Arthur passed away. In which case, she'll have grown up without human contact."

"So she's like a wildcat," James said.

Wilfred nodded.

Mandy bit her lip thoughtfully. If the cat really was wild, then it wasn't going to be easy to catch it. And it might even be a little dangerous. The poor thing might lash out if she was alarmed. "We really should call Betty Hilder," she said to James. "She'll know what's best."

"Is that the lady who runs the animal sanctuary on the other side of Welford?" asked Wilfred.

"That's right," said Mandy. "She often has stray cats

to look after. She might be able to come and help us with this one."

"Come into the house, then," said Wilfred. He led the way into the old-fashioned kitchen with its big white sink and oak dresser.

The phone was by the window, and a local phone book lay on the table beside it. James found the number for Welford Animal Sanctuary and read it aloud to Mandy.

She dialed the number, keeping her fingers crossed that Betty was in and could come out to Wilfred's place right away. The sooner those kittens were taken somewhere warm and safe, the better.

"Welford Animal Sanctuary," said a pleasant voice down the line.

That isn't Betty, Mandy thought, puzzled. "Can I speak to Betty Hilder, please?" she asked.

"I'm sorry, Betty's on vacation," came the reply. "My name is Diana and I'm looking after the animals while she is away. Can I help you?"

Mandy thought rapidly. This lady sounded friendly, but would she be able to deal with a wildcat? "My name is Mandy Hope," she explained. "I've found a stray cat and her three kittens, and I wanted to ask if Betty could come and get them."

"Oh, I don't think I can take any more animals while Betty isn't here," Diana said apologetically. "I'm rushed off my feet as it is. I'm really sorry, but I just can't help you. Betty will be back next week — maybe you could try her then." Mandy heard a scuffle in the background. "Oh, no!" Diana exclaimed. "One of Betty's dogs has just knocked the cookie jar off the table. I have to go. Good-bye." The phone went dead.

Mandy's heart sank. Those kittens couldn't stay outside for another week! She noticed James looking anxiously at her.

"Betty's on vacation!" she told him in dismay. "There's a lady called Diana looking after the animals, but she doesn't want to take in any more animals while Betty is away."

"Would your parents be able to help?" asked James.

"They might, if they know Betty can't," Mandy replied. She glanced at her watch. It was mid-morning; her parents would both be out on their rounds now. "They won't be there at the moment though."

"Well, come and see Matty first, then," Wilfred offered. "She'd like a visit."

Mandy and James followed Wilfred out of the yard and through the gate that led into the campsite. The spaces where the tents had been pitched the summer before were now empty. But since they'd last visited, a number of old-fashioned wooden caravans had been added to the site, each freshly painted in a bright color.

"I like the trailers," James commented.

"Me, too," Mandy agreed. "Though I'd have thought Sam Western would have gone for something really up-to-date," she added. Sam Western was a local dairy farmer who owned a lot of land in the area. His farming methods were very modern and his barns were always filled with the latest machinery.

A smile caught at the corners of Wilfred's lips. "Yes, I was surprised, too," he said. "But then I spoke to the man delivering them, and he said that Mr. Western had been offered them all as part of a business deal. He got them for a first-rate price apparently. . . ."

"That explains it then." James grinned. "Sam Western never passes up an opportunity to make money."

"Even if it's at the expense of animals," Mandy said, her eyes darkening as she remembered the time that Sam Western had almost caused a herd of deer to be destroyed because he had wanted to cut down and sell the trees in the forest where they lived.

"Yes, he's certainly not overly fond of animals," Wilfred agreed. "It's lucky that cat didn't bring her kittens here. A few months ago, he found a couple of other cats living in the campsite shower room. I've never seen anyone so angry. He got rid of them right away."

"Got rid of them?" Mandy asked in alarm. "How?"

"A man took them away," Wilfred replied. "Said he

was going to 'deal with them' for Mr. Western. I didn't like the sound of it at all."

Mandy shivered. She and James had had several run-ins with Sam Western in the past when he had tried to "deal with" animals. "Yes, thank goodness the gray cat came to you instead, Wilfred," she agreed.

Wilfred nodded, then lifted his fingers to his lips. He whistled shrilly. They heard a distant whinny, and a few seconds later a silver-gray mare came cantering over the hill toward them.

"Matty!" Mandy exclaimed in delight.

The gray mare stopped in front of them. She nuzzled Wilfred's gnarled hands before turning and giving Mandy and James a friendly sniff. Mandy took the apple out of her pocket. "Here, girl," she said, offering it from her open palm.

"She'll be glad when the campground opens again at Easter, won't you, girl?" Wilfred said, as Matty crunched happily on the apple. "She's been getting bored with nothing to do."

Smiling, Mandy nodded. When the campground was open, Matty gave rides to the children who stayed there. They loved her.

"But I'm going to have to get her fit again first," Wilfred went on. "I haven't ridden her much over the winter. My back's been laying me up." An idea suddenly seemed to strike him. "I don't suppose you two would be able to give me a hand getting her fit again, would you? If you like, you could take her out for a few rides."

"Oh, yes!" Mandy gasped, her eyes shining.

"Definitely!" James agreed. Though he wasn't quite as eager to ride as Mandy, he loved riding gentle old Matty. "We're on spring break all week so we could come up each day, Wilfred."

Wilfred smiled. "Well, that would be great."

Mandy hugged the gentle mare. "Oh, Matty!" she said. "Did you hear that? We're going to have such fun!"

Two

"I hope Mom or Dad's here," Mandy said, as she and James biked into the Animal Ark driveway later that morning.

Simon, Animal Ark's young veterinary nurse, was stacking up boxes of worming medication behind the reception desk. "Hi," he said cheerfully as they entered.

"Are Mom and Dad back, Simon?" Mandy asked.

"Nope, they're both still out," Simon replied. "Your mom rang to say she'd been held up at Grove Farm, but your dad should be here soon." Then, seeing Mandy's face fall, he added, "What's up? Can I help?"

"I don't know," Mandy sighed. She explained about the gray cat and her kittens, and the fact that Betty Hilder couldn't help because she was on vacation.

Simon looked concerned. "Kittens are very vulnerable to disease at such a young age. They need to be put somewhere warm as quickly as possible."

"Uh-huh, that's what we thought," Mandy said, even more worried now that Simon had confirmed her fears for the kittens.

Just then, the door opened and Adam Hope came into the clinic, wearing his farm clothes: green padded jacket, thick trousers, and rubber boots. In one hand he carried a cardboard box. His blue eyes took in the little group by the reception desk. "What's all this about?" he asked. "You three look as thick as thieves."

"Dad!" Mandy exclaimed. "There's a stray cat up at Wilfred's with three kittens!" She quickly repeated the story. ". . . And because Betty can't help, we *have* to, Dad!" she finished.

Dr. Adam thought for a few seconds, then nodded. "I think we should go up there early tomorrow, before the morning clinic," he decided.

Simon nodded. "You can count me in, too."

"And me," said James.

"Thanks, Dad!" Mandy cried. She gave her father a hug. "But how are we going to catch the mother?" she asked worriedly. "We have to persuade her that we don't want to hurt her or her kittens."

"Could we tame her by leaving food out for her?" James suggested. "That's what we did with Blossom." Blossom was another stray cat turned feral whom they had once helped.

Dr. Adam rubbed his beard. "I think we need a faster solution, James," he replied. "If the kittens are cold, then the sooner we can get them inside the better."

"And there's always the danger that the mother might feel threatened by attempts to tame her and decide to move the kittens somewhere else," Simon added.

Dr. Adam nodded. "If enough of us go, we should be able to corner her. We can win her trust later, when she and her kittens are safe." Then he looked at his watch. "Well, now that's sorted out, how about we have some lunch?" he said, holding up a cardboard box. "You'll stay, won't you, James? I can offer you homemade vegetable potpies straight from Sam Western's new organic farm!"

"Sam Western's got an organic farm?" Mandy said in surprise. "Since when?"

"He's owned it for a couple of months," her dad replied. "He doesn't run it himself — he has a tenant farmer. But I think he saw that there was money to be made in organic produce. The farm stand certainly charged me enough for these potpies. Still, they look delicious."

Mandy grinned and patted her father's rather portly stomach. "You think all food looks delicious!"

"I shall ignore that comment," her dad said with mock dignity. "Now, who wants some lunch?"

The potpies *were* delicious. After lunch, Mandy and James helped clear the plates away and then biked back to Wilfred's. They took with them a piece of sheepskin bedding and more newspaper for the kittens, and some extra-nutritious formula cat food for the mother. But when they knocked on Wilfred's door, there was no answer.

"He must have gone out," James said. "Let's take the stuff around to the backyard for the cat."

"At least the sheepskin should keep the kittens warm tonight," Mandy commented as they walked into the yard.

The mother cat was prowling around by the entrance to the passageway when they arrived, but as soon as she saw them she flattened her ears and shot away.

"She's so skinny," James said, watching her streak across the road.

"It can't have been easy for her trying to feed three

kittens and catch food for herself," Mandy said, her heart going out to the young creature.

While James hung on to Blackie, Mandy edged down the passageway with the sheepskin. The kittens seemed pleased to see her. As she crouched down to say hello, they tumbled out of their newspaper nest and walked unsteadily toward her, meowing.

Mandy stroked each of them in turn. With one tiny paw, the adventurous black kitten began to play with the laces on her sneakers. However, he didn't quite have the balance to stand on three legs and he tumbled over in a small furry heap. Mandy laughed and scooped

him up into her arms. "You are a little cutie," she said, kissing him on his nose. He stared at her for a moment with his big blue eyes and then meowed loudly.

Although Mandy could have happily sat there and played with the kittens for hours, she knew she had work to do. Putting the black kitten down, she set about clearing away the soiled and damp newspaper and then laid down the piece of sheepskin bedding, with more clean newspaper on top. "It's only for one more night," she promised the kittens. "Tomorrow we'll take you somewhere safe and dry." Then she scooped up the dirty newspaper, carried it out of the passageway, and put it into Wilfred's trash can.

"Now, we'll just leave the mother's food out nearby," James said. "And hopefully she'll find it when she comes back."

When everything was done, Mandy wrote a note for Wilfred saying they would be back early the next morning and then biked back with James to Animal Ark.

They arrived just as the afternoon clinic was starting and the waiting room was filling up with patients. Several people were lined up at the desk talking to Jean Knox, the gray-haired receptionist. Eager to say hello to everyone, Blackie lunged forward, his tongue hanging out and tail wagging.

"I'd better take him home," James said, struggling to hang on to the excitable Labrador. "What time should I come around tomorrow?"

"Meet us here at six-thirty, so Mom and Dad can come with us before the morning clinic," Mandy said.

"Six-thirty!" James groaned. "That's so early!"

"Of course, you don't have to come —" Mandy began.

"No, no. I'll be here," James said hastily.

Mandy grinned. She'd known that, despite his moaning, James wouldn't miss the morning's adventure for anything. "See you then," she said.

As James left, Mandy hurried through to the office and slipped on her white coat. She loved helping in the clinic. There were lots of things to do — helping to hold and comfort patients, fetching medicine for her mom and dad, wiping down the examination tables with disinfectant — not to mention mopping up puddles on the floor. . . .

Although Mandy was busy, she found time to drop by the residential unit to see how Dylan was. The puppy was still lying quietly in his cage without moving. Mandy checked his water and stroked him for a little while before going back into the clinic.

Just as she came out of the residential unit, her mom appeared at the door of one of the examination rooms.

"Hello, love," she said. "Have you got a moment? Simon's in with Dad and I could use an extra pair of hands."

"Sure," Mandy said eagerly. She followed her mom into the examination room. A woman and a young girl were standing next to the examination table. On top of it was a rabbit carrier.

"I need to put some eyedrops in," Dr. Emily explained. "If you could just help to hold him, Mandy. He's being a bit frisky."

Mandy nodded and watched her mom flip open the lid of the carrier.

The cream-colored rabbit inside struggled wildly in Dr. Emily's arms when she took him out. But, gradually, he began to calm down a little.

"Fluffy's got sore eyes," the little girl told Mandy.

"That's right," Dr. Emily said, smiling at her. "It's called conjunctivitis. But these drops should make him feel better soon." She gave the rabbit to Mandy to hold.

He bucked a little, but Mandy knew how to hold on firmly but gently. She watched her mom squeeze the drops into Fluffy's eyes. He blinked but kept calm in Mandy's arms. "All done," she told him gently, and then she put him back in his carrier.

Dr. Emily explained about Fluffy's medicine to the girl's mother and then she showed them out of the examination room, leaving Mandy to wipe the table.

"Archie Austin," Mandy heard her mom call into the waiting room.

A moment later, her mom reappeared with an elderly woman leading a brown-and-white springer spaniel. He was walking slowly and the dark hair around his muzzle was heavily flecked with gray.

"So what's wrong with Archie, Mrs. Austin?" Dr. Emily asked, shutting the door.

Mrs. Austin looked worried. "Well, he's been limping on his front left leg for a while," she began. "I thought it was just arthritis because he's sixteen years old now, but it seems to be getting worse."

Dr. Emily lifted Archie onto the consulting table and began to run her hands over his legs. "There is a little lump here," she said, her experienced fingers probing Archie's left leg above his ankle. "Have you noticed any other changes in his behavior?"

"Well, he's been very quiet over the last few weeks and he's also not eating his food," Mrs. Austin replied. "I know he's old, but he's always been so healthy until now."

Dr. Emily nodded. "OK, I'll just give him a general checkup. Mandy, can you hold his head, please?"

Mandy moved up to the table and gently but firmly took hold of Archie on either side of his head. "Good boy," she told him. He looked up at her with deep, trusting eyes while her mom checked his glands, looked in his mouth, listened to his heart, and took his temperature.

Finally, Dr. Emily straightened up and rubbed Archie's head. "I think I'm going to need to X-ray him, Mrs. Austin," she said. "The lameness could just be the result of a knock or arthritis, but I need to check that it's nothing more serious. At his age, we can't rule out the possibility of a bone tumor."

Mrs. Austin swallowed. "If anything happened to Archie, I don't know what I'd do," she said, her voice shaking slightly. "Since my husband died last year, he's been my best friend."

Seeing Mrs. Austin's distress, Mandy felt awful. She stroked Archie's ears and the little spaniel licked her hand.

Dr. Emily looked at Mrs. Austin sympathetically. "Please try not to worry too much," she said. "Like I said, it may not be anything serious." She turned to the computer on the side table and studied the appointments for the next few days. "We can X-ray him on Wednesday morning, if that's all right for you."

Mrs. Austin nodded.

"Bring him in at eight-thirty in the morning," Dr. Emily said. "You'll be able to get him that afternoon but he'll be a bit wobbly from the anesthetic. Do you have someone who can give you a ride?"

Mrs. Austin nodded. "My son. He brought me in to-day."

"Good," Dr. Emily said. She patted Archie. "Well, we'll see you then. Mandy, can you show Mrs. Austin out?"

Mandy nodded and held the door open for Mrs. Austin and Archie. Despite her mom's words, Mrs. Austin's face was lined with worry. Mandy felt her heart twist as she watched the spaniel walking stiffly beside his owner. It was horrible seeing animals get old. "Bye, Archie," she said softly. "See you on Wednesday."

When the clinic finished, Mandy helped Simon mop the floors and clean the surfaces for the next day, and then she went through to the residential unit to see Dylan.

The puppy still lay on his stomach, his ears flopping sadly. Mandy kneeled down beside him and stroked his head. "Poor boy," she said. "You still don't look very happy."

Just then, the door opened and Simon came in. "How is he?" he asked.

"Just the same," Mandy replied. "Is he paralyzed, Simon?" She had seen cats and dogs after road accidents who had sustained such injuries to their spine that their legs would no longer work, and she wondered if that would be the case with Dylan.

"No," Simon said. He picked up one of Dylan's big

white paws. "His pads are warm and look . . ." He pinched the skin between Dylan's toes. After a few seconds the puppy moved his foot away. "His reflexes are slower than normal but he can still react to pain. If he was paralyzed he wouldn't be able to move his paw at all."

Mandy sighed with relief.

Then Simon put his hands under the puppy and gently tried to lift him into a standing position. But Dylan's legs refused to carry his weight, and Simon let the puppy flop back down. "He should be ready to stand and move by now, though," Simon observed, frowning. "He's going to have to show some more progress soon in order to have chance of a full recovery. If not, your mom and dad might advise that it would be kindest to put him to sleep. . . ."

Mandy gasped in shock. She looked at the pup's sad face. He looked really depressed. "Have his owners been to see him yet?" she asked.

Simon shook his head. "Your dad advised them not to come in until Dylan had recovered a little, in case he got too excited," Simon replied. "But they've already called three times today to see how he is — they're obviously really worried."

Mandy looked at the puppy. "Maybe he's just missing them. It must be really strange for him being away from his home."

Simon patted Dylan. "Maybe." He stood up. "Well, I'd better get going. I'll see you tomorrow, about six-thirty, for a little cat catching."

"Yeah, see you then," Mandy replied.

The door shut behind Simon, and Mandy was left on her own with Dylan. She sat stroking him for a long time.

Mandy's alarm clock woke her up at a quarter to six the next morning. It was still dark outside and she could hear a light rain pattering on her window. Her heart sank — the kittens! The sooner they got them warm and dry the better. She threw back the covers and leaped out of bed.

Her mom was already in the kitchen, filling the kettle to make coffee. "Have you got everything we need for catching these cats?" she asked. Dr. Emily had volunteered to help, too.

Mandy nodded. The night before she had gotten out two cat carriers, some food, a bowl, several thick blankets, and five pairs of sturdy gloves. The plan was to put the food down and then catch the mother cat while she was eating, throwing a blanket over her so that she couldn't scratch them or escape. With five pairs of hands, they hoped they could block all the escape routes. Mandy knew that the cat would be frightened, but as she looked at the rain falling outside she knew that they had to do it. If the weather worsened, then the kittens might not survive.

At six-thirty, everyone assembled in warm coats and scarves in the waiting room.

James came in last, yawning loudly and looking bleary-eyed. "I can't believe I got up this early," he grumbled as they all climbed into the Hopes' Land Rover.

"Just think of the cat and her kittens," Mandy said, handing him a carrier to hold.

"Now, we'll need to be quiet when we get there," Dr. Adam warned them. "We don't want the mother being frightened and running off. Mandy, I suggest that you go into the yard and leave the food near the entrance to the passageway. Simon, you and James block off the yard gate. Emily and I will stay near the back of the yard and move in once the cat is eating."

Dawn was just breaking as they reached Wilfred's cottage. Dr. Emily handed out the gloves and then they all quietly got out of the Land Rover. The rain had stopped and the air seemed still and quiet. No one said a word.

Mandy took the bowl of food and cautiously opened the gate. It creaked slightly. The noise seemed very loud and Mandy froze for a moment, holding her breath. But nothing happened. After a few seconds, she began to breathe again. She crept forward, her eyes adjusting to the dim light. As she crossed the yard, she could hear the faint sounds of the others moving into position behind her.

She reached the entrance to the passageway. Putting down the food bowl, she peered into the darkness. The white sheepskin bedding was just visible at the end. Mandy stared. The nest was deserted.

The cat and her kittens were gone!

Three

Mandy looked around. "They're not here!" she called out. The others came forward, looking surprised.

"The mother cat must have moved them," her mom groaned, looking down the passageway. "I guess all the activity yesterday must have been too much for her. Feral cats do sometimes move their young to a new nest if they feel threatened."

Mandy stared at her. "So she moved them because of us?"

Her mom put an arm around her shoulders. "Don't blame yourself. You were only trying to help."

"What will happen to the kittens?" James asked. His

voice was shaky and Mandy was sure that, despite her mom's comforting words, he felt as bad as she did. It was awful to think the cat had moved her family because of their interference.

"It all depends where they've gone," Dr. Emily said. "If it's somewhere safe and dry, then they'll be OK."

"They might not have gone far," Simon said hopefully. "We could look for them."

"I guess it's worth a try," Dr. Adam agreed.

They started searching the rest of the yard and the hedgerows outside.

They had been looking for ten minutes when Wilfred came out of his house. "What's going on?" he asked, looking at the search party in surprise.

Feeling terrible, Mandy explained.

Wilfred's face fell. "Poor little mites," he said. "They were there when I went to bed last night. I went out to check on them. Here, I'll get my coat and help you look. There's a grove of trees down the road. Maybe they've gone there."

He went into the house and reappeared a minute later wearing a heavy coat, then led the way to the woods.

"We have to find them," Mandy said desperately to James. She kept imagining the kittens huddling together, cold and damp, on a bed of leaves.

James nodded, his eyes anxious behind his glasses.

"The weather's supposed to get colder tonight. I heard it on the TV. They were saying that there might be a frost."

Feeling worse than ever, Mandy began to search. She looked under bushes, in hollow tree trunks, in piles of leaves — but there was no sign of the kittens.

At a quarter to eight, Dr. Adam and Dr. Emily shook their heads. "We're going to have to stop looking," Dr. Emily said.

"We can't!" Mandy protested.

"We have to, love," said her mom. "Dad and I have got to prepare for the morning clinic."

"I'm sorry, Mandy, but I have to stop as well," said Wilfred. "Matty will be wondering where her breakfast is!"

"Well, we'll stay and keep looking," James said, looking at Mandy. "There's more places to check — there's the campground for a start."

"You must be very careful if you see these cats," Dr. Adam warned. "The mother cat might panic if you try to catch her and she'll scratch and bite if she thinks her kittens are in danger. Try to get her used to you by giving her some food. Then she might let you pick her up, but don't forget to wear the gloves!"

"OK, Dad, we'll be really careful," Mandy promised. "Come on, James, let's get going!"

"Oh — and what about breakfast? You haven't eaten yet," Dr. Emily suddenly remembered.

"Breakfast!" Mandy echoed. She couldn't even think about food with the kittens missing.

"Tell you what," Wilfred said suddenly. "I can rustle up a few sandwiches for these two later on, no problem."

"Oh, yes, please!" Mandy said, looking pleadingly at her mom.

"OK," Dr. Emily agreed. "I'll call your house, James, and let your parents know what's happening. But don't get your hopes too high. The cat could have gone anywhere."

After waving Dr. Adam, Dr. Emily, and Simon off, Mandy and James hurried to the campsite. "I don't know whether I want the cat to be here or not," James panted as they ran across the field to the shower room. "You know what Wilfred said yesterday about Sam Western getting rid of those cats."

Mandy remembered only too well. "If she *is* here we'll just have to move her before he finds out," she said firmly.

They searched every inch of the shower room. Behind the wooden partition at one end, they could hear Matty shifting in the straw.

"Let's try Matty's stable and feed storage room," Mandy said.

Matty greeted Mandy and James with a soft whinny. Mandy went up and stroked her velvety gray nose. However, it didn't take long to see that Matty was the only animal in the stable area. There was no sign of the cat or her kittens.

"Let's go and check under the trailers," James said.

They were just leaving the stable when Wilfred appeared with a thermos of tea and some sandwiches. "Any sign of the kittens?" he asked.

"No," Mandy replied. "We're going to look around the caravans."

"Well, you'd better be quick," Wilfred said. "Sam Western's coming up here sometime today. I think he's planning on getting the campsite ready to open again. You don't want him to catch sight of the cat if she's here."

"No, we don't," Mandy said in alarm. "Come on, James!"

They ran over to the caravans and checked quickly underneath them.

"Nothing," James said at last, as they walked unhappily back to the stable.

Wilfred had brought Matty out and was tying her up outside so that he could clean her stall. "Cup of tea?" he offered, looking at their faces.

Mandy and James shook their heads.

"Now don't you fret," Wilfred said kindly. "That cat's been living in the wild for some time now. She'll know how to look after herself. Why don't you take a break from all this searching and give me a hand with Matty? You ought to have something to eat, too."

Mandy looked at James. She didn't want to give up looking for the cat, but where else was there to look? They seemed to have searched everywhere.

James shrugged. "OK," he said to Wilfred.

"Great," Wilfred said. "Matty could do with a brush over."

After finishing the sandwiches, Mandy and James got the grooming kit from the feed storage room and set to work. As Mandy brushed Matty's face, the mare nuzzled her gently. It was as if she could sense Mandy's distress.

"What are we going to do?" James asked.

"I don't know," Mandy replied. "We've got to find her." She moved around to brush Matty's tail and suddenly gasped. Running across the field was the gray cat. "James!" she cried. "Look!"

But by the time James had turned, the cat had disappeared through the hedge. "What am I looking for?" he asked, confused.

"It was the cat!" Mandy exclaimed. "Come on!" Throwing down the grooming brush she was using, she set off across the field.

"Are you sure?" James panted as they ran through the long grass.

"Positive," Mandy said. They reached the hedge. "She must have gone through here." Bending down, she pointed to a gap just large enough for the cat to have squeezed through.

James looked over to the other side of the hedge, where a field stretched out. "She could be anywhere," he said, looking around the empty open space.

Mandy knew he was right. "At least we know she's

somewhere nearby," she said, thinking fast. "We'll have to keep watch for when she comes through here again. Then, when she does, we can follow her to the kittens."

James nodded, fixing his glasses more firmly on his nose. "And let's leave some food out for her nearby," he suggested.

"Good idea," Mandy agreed.

They hurried back to Wilfred's cottage and got the bowl of food they'd brought from Animal Ark.

"Sam Western's not going to like this," James said, as they placed the bowl near the hedge.

"So we can't let him find out," Mandy said. "Luckily, the caravans are nowhere near here, so he might not even come this way." But just to be on the safe side she arranged some long grass around the bowl so that it couldn't be seen from a distance. "Now all we need to do is to watch it," she said.

"We could go on grooming Matty while we wait," James suggested.

They went back up to Matty and finished brushing her, all the time keeping one eye on the hole in the hedge and the feed bowl nearby.

At last, Matty's gray coat was clean and her mane and tail were silky and tangle free.

Wilfred came out of the stable. He smiled at Mandy and James. "You've done a good job there," he remarked.

"We've enjoyed it," Mandy said, and she meant it. Ever since she had caught that fleeting glimpse of the cat, she had been feeling much happier. She was sure that they would find the kittens now. It was just a case of waiting.

"Now how about riding Matty for me?" Wilfred suggested.

Mandy looked at James.

"We might as well," he said. "We can still watch out for the cat and, anyway, it might be ages before she comes back."

They got Matty's tack from the storeroom and each picked a riding hat that Wilfred kept for the campers to use.

"Just take it gently," Wilfred said, as Mandy pulled down the stirrup and prepared to mount. "I've got some cleaning up to do in the house so I'll leave you to it. When you've finished, give her a rubdown and turn her loose."

Mandy nodded, then swung herself into the saddle. It felt wonderful to be on Matty again. "You keep watch while I ride," she said to James, "then we can swap."

"OK," he agreed.

Mandy rode Matty down the field. The obedient mare walked, trotted, and cantered exactly when Mandy asked. "You're such a lovely old girl, Matty," Mandy told her, patting her smooth neck. And Matty tossed her head as if she understood.

Half an hour later, Mandy and James untacked Matty and rubbed her down.

"That was fun," Mandy said, smiling happily as they turned Matty loose in the field. The mare immediately put her head down and started to graze.

"Still no sign of the cat, though," James said, glancing toward the bowl. "Hey!" he said, grabbing Mandy's arm. "Look!"

Mandy swung around. It was the cat! Crouching nervously by the food bowl, she was eating big, hungry mouthfuls. "Quick!" Mandy exclaimed.

They began to hurry around the outside of the field. As they drew nearer, James slowed down. "We mustn't upset her," he hissed to Mandy. "We don't want her running away again."

Mandy nodded and they began to creep toward the cat as quietly as they could. *If we can just get near enough to follow her. . . .* Mandy thought. She could feel her heart beating quickly in her chest. The cat mustn't escape from them again.

Just then, the cat finished the food and looked up. Mandy and James froze but the cat didn't seem to notice them. With a shake of her head, she began trotting purposefully up the field.

"Where's she going?" Mandy whispered, in surprise. She had expected the cat to go back through the hedge.

"I don't know," replied James. "Let's follow her."

Keeping a safe distance, they began to run quietly after the thin gray shape.

"She's heading for the caravans," Mandy said suddenly.

Veering to the left, the cat made a beeline for the trailer farthest away from the campsite entrance. Reaching it, she trotted around to the back.

A moment later, Mandy and James stopped beside the bright orange caravan. They looked all around but the cat had vanished.

"Look!" James whispered, pointing at the side of the trailer. One of the planks of wood had come loose and there was a gap just big enough for a cat to squeeze through. "Maybe she's inside."

Very cautiously, they stole across the grass to the caravan window. It was high up, but by standing on the wheel, Mandy could just see inside. Her heart leaped. "She's in there!" she whispered excitedly to James.

The cat was standing in the middle of the trailer and her kittens were stumbling around her. Mandy got down so that James could climb onto the wheel and have a look, too. "They're all there," he said, breathing out in relief.

Suddenly, a horrible thought struck Mandy. "But what about Sam Western?" she gasped. "Remember he's coming to check out the caravans today. If he finds the kittens . . ." Her voice trailed off as she stared at James.

The relief drained from his face. "You know what Wilfred said happened to those other cats," James said slowly. He jumped off the wheel onto the ground.

"We can't let Sam Western find them here, James!" Mandy exclaimed.

"But what can we do?" he said in dismay. "We can't get into the trailer."

Mandy looked at the shut window and the locked door. James was right. There was no way in except through the gap in the side and that was far too small for a person to get through. For a moment, Mandy thought wildly about breaking the window, but even if they did that, how would they get the cat out? She was so scared of humans that it was going to be very difficult to catch her. Mandy made a decision. "Let's go and call Mom and Dad from Wilfred's house," she said. "See what they say."

"But what if the cat's heard us?" James said. "What if she moves the kittens while we're gone? Or what if Sam Western comes?"

Mandy hadn't thought of that. She bit her lip anxiously.

"Look, I'll stay and keep watch. You go," James said, looking determined. "But be quick!"

"OK!" Mandy gasped. She set off across the field as fast as she could go. By the time she reached Wilfred's door, her heart was pounding and her breath was coming in short gasps. Panting loudly, she banged the knocker hard. *Please hurry, Wilfred!* she thought.

Wilfred opened the door. His eyes took in her frantic face. "Whatever's the matter, Mandy?" he demanded.

"The cats — they're in one of the caravans —" Gradually, Mandy found enough breath to gasp out the whole story. "Can I use your phone, Wilfred?" she asked. "I want to ring Mom and Dad."

"Of course," Wilfred said. "You know where it is."

Mandy hurried through the kitchen to the phone. Grabbing the receiver, she dialed the Animal Ark number.

Jean Knox answered almost at once, but to Mandy's dismay she couldn't help. "I'm sorry, Mandy, love," Jean said, "but your dad's out on his rounds and your mom's in the operating room with Simon. I can give her a message when she's finished."

"Can you tell her that we've found the cat and her kittens, please?" Mandy said desperately. "But they're in one of the trailers and Sam Western's coming. We don't know what to do."

"I'll tell her," Jean promised.

Mandy put the phone down, feeling frustrated and helpless.

"Now, now, Mandy," said Wilfred sympathetically. "Don't you go getting so upset. We'll get those cats out. You just go and get the stuff you brought this morning."

"But how will we get into the caravan?" Mandy asked.

Wilfred tapped his nose. "Leave that to me."

A ray of hope suddenly lightened Mandy's despair. If Wilfred could open the trailer, then maybe she and James *would* be able to get the cats out by themselves. She raced outside and picked up the cat food and gloves that her mom and dad had left.

Soon, she and Wilfred were hurrying across the field. In one hand, Wilfred swung a metal bar that was flattened at one end. "This should be just what we need," he'd said as he produced it from his old wooden toolbox in the hall.

As they neared the orange caravan, Mandy broke into a run.

"I thought you were never coming back!" James exclaimed. His face was anxious. "Did you speak to your mom and dad?"

Mandy shook her head. "I couldn't. They were both busy. But Wilfred's going to help. He thinks he can open the caravan door." She dumped the cat carriers, gloves, blankets, and food on the grass. "We're going to have to catch the cat ourselves."

James looked thoughtful. "Before we go in, we should block off the loose plank so that the cat can't escape that way," he said quickly. "Let's get a bale of hay."

Mandy only just stopped herself from hugging him. That was the best thing about James; when there was an animal in trouble he never stopped thinking of ways to help it.

Leaving Wilfred to examine the door, Mandy and James fetched a bale of hay from the stable. They struggled back across the grass with it and wedged it against the side of the caravan so that it blocked off the loose plank.

"Right! I think I can get this door open," Wilfred said, looking at them.

Mandy remembered her dad telling her that if the cat was frightened she would scratch and bite. She handed James a pair of gloves. "We'd better put these on," she said.

"What did your mom and dad say this morning about catching them?" James asked.

"Well, we want to try and keep her as calm as possible," Mandy said. "If she panics she'll be impossible to catch. One of us should go in and put some food on the floor. Then, as she's eating, we'll try and pick her up and get her into a carrier." Mandy bit her lip. She knew that the cat would hate being confined in the carrier, but if they were going to help her, then it was the only thing to do. She hoped that once they had the cat in a safe place they could teach her that humans were kind and not to be feared.

James nodded and picked up the food.

"Are you ready?" Wilfred asked.

Mandy took a deep breath and picked up the carriers. "We're ready," she said.

Wilfred picked up the metal bar.

"Hey!" An irate voice rang out behind them.

Mandy swung around. A smart, black Land Rover had drawn into the campsite. The driver's door was open and a stocky, fair-haired man wearing a green jacket was striding toward them. His face was red with anger. "Sam Western!" Mandy gasped to James.

Four

"Just what do you think you are doing?" Sam Western demanded furiously. As he reached the trailer, his thunderous blue eyes took in Mandy and James. "You two!" he exclaimed. "What are you troublemakers doing here?" He glared at Wilfred. "And what are you doing with my caravan?"

Wilfred looked like he didn't know what to say. He flushed to the roots of his white hair. "Well, er, it's like this, Mr. Western," he began.

"It's our fault," Mandy broke in quickly. She didn't want Wilfred to get into trouble. If Sam Western wanted to, he could order Wilfred to take Matty off the campsite.

49

"We asked Wilfred to help us," James said, backing Mandy up.

"Help you do what?" Sam Western exploded. "Break into one of my caravans?"

"We had to!" Mandy burst out. "There's a cat inside!"

For a moment there was silence. Sam Western stared at her as if he couldn't believe what she was saying. "There's a *what*?" he said, speaking very slowly.

"A cat," James said. "And her kittens. We were trying to get them out."

"Cats!" Sam Western's face creased with a look of repulsion. "We'll soon see about that!" He pulled a bunch of keys from his pocket and, pushing Mandy and James out of the way, strode to the trailer door.

Mandy leaped after him. "Please don't frighten them," she gasped. "The kittens are only tiny and the cat will panic."

"Mr. Western," Wilfred put in, "please be reasonable. . . ."

But Sam Western ignored them. Turning the key in the lock, he wrenched open the door and marched up the steps.

"Quick, James!" Mandy cried. "Get ready to catch them if they come out!"

As they leaped toward the open door, they heard Sam Western shout, "Right! Come here, you!"

They heard a hiss and a yowl — and then Sam Western started yelling.

Mandy's hands flew to her mouth. What was going on?

The next instant, Sam Western came staggering backward out of the caravan. One hand was clutching the other. "It attacked me!" he cried, blood oozing from his injured hand.

Mandy stood rooted to the spot in shock but James, showing great presence of mind, darted up the steps and slammed the door shut. "Now they can't escape!" he gasped to Mandy.

"Escape!" Sam Western echoed. "You're worried about the cat? It just attacked me!"

"Well, what did you expect?" Mandy cried. "She thought you were trying to take her kittens! She was just defending them."

"Defending them!" Sam Western spat. "We'll soon see about that." Shaking with rage, he turned and stormed toward his Land Rover.

Mandy felt a cold shiver of fear run down her spine. She raced after him. "What are you going to do?" she gasped.

"I'm going to get my hand taken care of, then I'm going to get someone to deal with those cats," Sam Western told her grimly.

"What do you mean?" Mandy cried in alarm.

But Sam Western didn't answer her. He had reached his Land Rover and he jumped in.

"Please, Mr. Western!" Mandy exclaimed, grabbing the door before he could shut it. "We'll move them for you. We'll take them away." Her mind raced. "And it won't waste your men's time!"

Sam Western glared at her. The deep scratch marks stood out vividly on his left hand but the mention of saving time seemed to have gotten his attention. "You've got until lunchtime," he snapped. "If they're not gone by one o'clock, I'm getting someone in to do it."

He slammed the door shut and then drove off, revving the Land Rover's powerful engine noisily as he sped across the grass.

James came running up to Mandy. "What's happening?" he demanded.

Mandy turned around, her face pale. "We've got until one o'clock to move the cats. Come on!"

Although both Mandy and James wanted to get straight back into the caravan and catch the cats, they knew they had to be patient. The mother cat was going to be terrified after her encounter with Sam Western, and so they decided to give the cat half an hour to calm down. To help pass the time, they cleaned Matty's saddle and bridle for Wilfred.

"What are we going to do if we can't catch the mother cat?" James said, as they rubbed damp sponges over the leather.

Mandy didn't even want to think about what would happen. "We'll get her out," she said, jutting out her chin in determination.

Just as they were finishing the tack, a white van drove into the campground. A group of workmen jumped out and began unloading some tools from the van.

"Take them over to the ditches," a sharp-faced man directed them. Mandy immediately recognized him as Dennis Saville, Sam Western's hard-hearted estate manager.

"They must be Sam Western's men come to clean up the campsite," she said, as the men started to carry the tools across the field.

"I hope they don't upset Matty," James said, watching the gray mare skitter out of the men's way.

Just then, Dennis Saville caught sight of them. He strode over. "What are you two doing here?" he demanded, his humorless features creasing into a frown. "This is private property."

"We're helping Wilfred," James said, holding up the bridle he had just finished putting back together.

"And we're trying to get a cat out of one of the caravans for Mr. Western," Mandy added, forcing herself to be polite. She didn't want Dennis Saville interfering. "She's living there with her kittens."

Dennis Saville's eyebrows rose. "A cat!" he said incredulously. "Oh-ho, the boss won't like that."

"He didn't," James muttered under his breath.

"Well, we're going to move her," Mandy continued bravely. "Then Mr. Western won't have to see her again."

"A stray, is she?" Dennis Saville asked.

Mandy and James nodded.

The estate manager gave a short laugh. "I might have known. You two are always running around the countryside interfering with things. Rescuing foxes one minute. Stray cats the next. If it was up to me, I'd get the boss's dogs and flush her out."

Mandy's temper snapped and she jumped to her feet. "Well, it's not up to you!" she exclaimed. "Mr. Western told us we could have until one o'clock to move her, so you'd better just leave her alone!"

Dennis Saville stepped toward her. "Or what?" he said menacingly.

James grabbed Mandy's arm. "We're only trying to help," he said quickly to Dennis Saville before Mandy could reply. "We'll move the cat."

"You'd better," Dennis Saville said. "Or I'll do it for you." He turned on his heel and strode away.

Infuriated beyond belief, Mandy struggled to get away from James but he hung on to her. "Calm down!" he urged. "It won't do the cats any good."

Mandy quickly realized that James was right. If they antagonized Dennis Saville, then maybe he would carry out his threat and fetch Sam Western's fierce bulldogs. She took a deep breath. "OK."

"Come on," James said. "Let's go and see if we can get that cat out."

Putting the saddle and bridle away, they went to the caravan. At the side of the field, the men were shouting to each other as they began to clear out the ditches. Mandy listened at the trailer door. It was quiet inside. "OK," she said, her heart beating fast. "Let's go in."

She pushed open the door just a crack, her hands ready to slam it shut if the cat tried to escape. She waited for the cat to yowl and leap. But nothing happened. Mandy put her eye to the crack. At first, it was too dark to see anything, but gradually her eyes adapted to the dim light. "I can see her," she whispered to James. "She's with the kittens at the back."

As quietly as she could, Mandy pushed the door open and slipped inside. James followed her, carrying the bowl of food, and quickly shut the door behind him. The air smelled strongly of cats. The only light filtered in through a chink in the curtains.

At the far end of the caravan, the mother cat had risen to her feet and was staring at them, her skinny gray back arched and the hair on her spine standing up. Her kittens were sleeping beside her on an old newspaper. Opening her mouth, she drew her lips back and hissed warningly.

James pushed the bowl of food as far as he could toward her.

"Let's sit down," Mandy whispered. "It'll make us seem less threatening."

They crouched down by the door. As the minutes ticked by, the hair on the cat's back gradually flattened but she didn't move. She stood over her kittens, her muscles tense, watching them with her large amber eyes.

"It's OK," Mandy murmured. "We won't hurt you." Wondering if she could get closer, she began to inch across the floor. The cat's hair immediately rose again and she spat loudly.

Mandy quickly moved back. The spitting sound woke the black kitten. Blinking sleepily, he saw Mandy and James and began to amble toward them. With one swift movement, the mother cat shot out her front paw and cuffed him soundly. He rolled over with a startled meow. Scrambling to his feet, he stumbled back to the newspaper and curled up beside his brother and sister.

"Poor thing!" Mandy whispered in distress.

"The mother's never going to let us anywhere near her," James whispered back. "She's not even looking at the food."

"She will," Mandy said optimistically. "She'll get used to us in the end."

But after an hour had passed and the cat had shown no sign of relaxing with them, even Mandy's spirits started to fall.

"Come on," James sighed. "This is getting us nowhere. "Let's go outside for a while."

They edged out of the caravan. The daylight seemed very bright after the gloomy interior. Dennis Saville had gone, but Sam Western's men were still there. They were throwing big piles of vegetation out of the ditches. Matty seemed to have lost her fear of them and was grazing nearby.

"What are we going to do?" asked Mandy, sinking down on the trailer steps and breathing in the fresh air.

James sat down beside her. "I don't know," he admitted.

"If we only had time to tame the mother cat," Mandy said despairingly.

"Well, we haven't." James looked at his watch. "It's

ten after twelve. We've got less than an hour." He ran a hand through his hair. "Look, I don't think we've got time to let the mother cat get used to us. We'll just have to get as close as we can and throw blankets over her so we can bundle her into the carrier. She won't like it, but it's better than being caught by Sam Western."

Mandy didn't want to frighten the cat but James was right — they were running out of time. "OK," she said reluctantly. "Let's get the blankets."

When they came back to the field, the workmen were packing up for lunch. Matty was still standing near them but she was no longer grazing. Mandy frowned. There was something about the mare that seemed odd.

"James," she said, stopping. "Look at Matty."

They both looked. Matty was standing absolutely still. Her neck was stretched out and all the muscles in her body looked stiff.

"She doesn't look well," Mandy said in alarm.

They hurried toward Matty, slowing down when they were a few yards away so as not to frighten her, but she hardly seemed to notice them.

"Matty?" said Mandy.

The mare continued to stare straight ahead.

Mandy went up to her and put a hand on her neck. Matty didn't even look around. The muscles under her skin were twitching. Fear shot through Mandy. What was the matter with her? "We'd better get Wilfred!" she gasped.

"I'll go," James said. "You stay here."

As James tore off, Mandy moved to the mare's head. Matty's pupils looked wide and dilated. Something was very definitely wrong. Mandy looked around. Was it something Matty had eaten? But how could it be? Wilfred was always very careful to check the field for poisonous plants. She stroked the mare's face. "It's OK, girl," Mandy murmured, desperately wishing that James and Wilfred would hurry up.

"Is everything all right?" One of the workmen passing nearby suddenly seemed to notice that something was wrong.

Mandy shook her head. "Matty's not well," she said. "But I don't know what's the matter."

The workman came over, his kindly face creasing in concern. "The old man owns her, doesn't he? Do you want me to get him?"

"My friend's just gone to get him," Mandy said.

"What's up, Bill?" one of the other workmen asked, coming over.

"The horse is ill," the man said.

Just then, to Mandy's relief, Wilfred and James appeared at the gate. "Wilfred!" she shouted. "Quick!"

Seeing Matty standing so stiffly, Wilfred started to run. By the time he reached her, he was wheezing loudly, his chest heaving with each breath. "Matty, girl!" he gasped.

At the sound of her owner's voice, the mare turned her head slightly, one ear flickering. But it was obvious that even a little movement was an effort for her. Wilfred's eye swept over her quivering skin, wide eyes, and stiff legs. "How long has she been like this?" he asked quickly.

"I don't know," Mandy replied anxiously. "We just noticed her when we were coming down the field. Do you know what the matter is?"

Wilfred's face was pale. "Yes," he replied, nodding. "It's poisoning. No doubt about it."

Five

Mandy, James, and the workmen stared at Wilfred.

"But how can it be poisoning?" Mandy blurted out. "You always check the field, Wilfred."

"I know," Wilfred said. "I don't know what she's eaten, but I know you don't get a horse looking like this unless it's been poisoned."

Matty took one faltering step forward and almost fell. James leaped beside Wilfred and together they managed to keep the mare on her feet by holding her halter firmly.

"Here, I'll help." Bill, the first workman, moved forward quickly.

"Do you want me to call a vet?" another workman offered. "We've got a phone in the van."

"Call Animal Ark!" Mandy exclaimed. "Tell them it's an emergency!" She reeled off the number, fear gripping her as she watched Matty stagger again. Whatever the poison was, it seemed to be acting very quickly.

The workman set off at a run across the field.

"Steady, girl!" Wilfred cried as Matty's legs shook. Mandy's heart contracted as she caught a glimpse of the mare's wide, frightened eyes. Matty seemed to be losing control of her muscles. *Hurry, please hurry!* she thought, watching the workman sprint up the field.

She turned back to the ill mare. "It's all right, Matty," she said desperately. "You're going to be OK."

The gray mare staggered again and Mandy felt her heart skip a beat. What if Matty didn't last until her mom or dad got here? What if the poison was too strong?

"Mandy! It's your mom!" James gasped.

Mandy swung around. Dr. Emily was walking through the campsite entrance. "Mom!" Mandy cried in relief. She suddenly realized that her mom must have got the message about the cats and decided to come by. "Mom! Quick! It's Matty! Wilfred thinks she's been poisoned!"

Dr. Emily broke into a run. In next to no time she had reached them. Her expert eyes swept over the mare's twitching muscles. "You're right, Wilfred," she said, moving forward to check Matty's gums and pupils. "It looks like poisoning. Something's affecting her nerve cells and stimulating her central nervous system. Let me get my bag." She ran back to the Land Rover.

Mandy stroked Matty with a trembling hand and forced herself to stay calm. Now that her mom was here, surely everything would be all right.

"Right," Dr. Emily said briskly as she came back and opened her bag. "I'm going to give her a shot of anticonvulsant to help stop the spasms in her muscles, but it's vital that we find out what the poison is." She turned to Wilfred. "Is there anything you can think of, Wilfred, that might have affected her like this?"

Wilfred shook his head. "I check the whole field regularly."

"When did her symptoms start?" Dr. Emily asked, taking a syringe and a vial of clear liquid out of her bag.

"It was Mandy and James who noticed her first," Wilfred replied.

"She was fine earlier on," Mandy said, remembering how Matty had been grazing happily when they had come out of the caravan. "She was eating near the workmen. But then James and I went to get the blankets from the house and, when we came back, we saw her looking ill."

Dr. Emily cleaned a square of hair on Matty's neck with a cotton ball and inserted the needle. The gray mare didn't even seem to notice. Dr. Emily injected the anticonvulsant medicine and turned to the workmen. "Have you been using anything on the grass?" she asked. "Any chemicals? Anything at all?"

Bill shook his head. "We've just been clearing out the ditches, that's all."

"The ditches?" Dr. Emily said quickly, glancing over to the piles of vegetation that the workmen had pulled up from the ditch around the side of the field. "Did you dig out any water hemlock?" The workman looked confused. "Cowbane is its other name. It's a tall, yellow-green plant with white flower heads and made up of lots of little flowers."

"Yeah, there was something like that," Bill said. "I thought it was just cow parsley. Tom, go and get some." The other workman ran across to the pile of vegetation by the ditches.

"Cowbane?" Wilfred said, looking shocked. "But that's deadly."

Dr. Emily nodded. "Its roots contain a toxic resin called cicutoxin that can be fatal to horses. It causes just the sort of symptoms Matty's got. It's my guess that when she was grazing near the ditches, she picked up some of the roots that had been dug out."

Just then, Tom returned with the plant. Its soil-covered roots showed white where the spades had cut through them. "Isn't this just cow parsley?" he asked.

"No," Dr. Emily said grimly. "It's from the parsley family but it's cowbane — much more dangerous to horses."

"Oh, Matty," Wilfred groaned.

"Will she be OK, Mom?" Mandy asked, her heart pounding.

Her mom's worried green eyes met hers. "I don't know, love," she said flatly. "It depends on how much she's eaten. If she's eaten a lot, then the muscular spasms will lead to respiratory paralysis, which means that she won't be able to breathe."

Mandy's heart clenched. "There must be something you can do," she said desperately.

"I can give her anticonvulsants to ease the spasms," Dr. Emily said. "But that's all. The next four to six hours will be crucial. If she survives those then there's every chance that she'll be OK."

"But she might not survive them?" Mandy whispered, her mouth dry.

"No," her mother said, taking a deep breath. "I'm afraid she might not."

The workmen stood around tensely, their lunch break forgotten. Dr. Emily had told everyone to let Matty lie down and now the mare lay on the grass, her big gray body covered by a rug. Her head was stretched out and her muscles twitched spasmodically under her skin.

Mandy crouched beside Matty's neck, stroking her over and over again. Her mom had done all that she could and now it was just a question of waiting to see if the drugs would take effect.

Wilfred cradled Matty's head in his lap. "I should have checked for cowbane in the ditches," he muttered, his voice cracking. "I could have kept her in her stable while the work was done."

"You didn't know," Dr. Emily said. "It was just one of those things, Wilfred."

"What would Rose say if she knew?" Wilfred whispered.

Mandy bit her lip as she saw the anguish in the old man's eyes. She knew that Matty had been his wife, Rose's, horse and it was partly because of this that the gray mare was so special to him. It was as though she still gave him a link with Rose. Mandy felt her own eyes sting with tears. *Please, Matty, get better*, she prayed desperately as she crouched beside Matty's neck.

Suddenly, a loud voice cut through the air. "What's all this about?"

Mandy looked up. Sam Western was striding toward them. Mandy realized with a jolt that it must be one o'clock. In the drama of the last hour, she had completely forgotten about the cat and her kittens.

"What's happened to the horse?" Sam Western demanded as he reached them. "Is it ill?"

Mandy couldn't bear his tone. Before anyone could speak, she scrambled to her feet and faced Sam Western, her eyes blazing. "Yes, she is!" she exclaimed. "And it's all your fault!"

"My fault?" Sam Western echoed, looking taken aback. "What on earth do you mean?"

"She ate some cowbane from the ditches," Mandy told him, knowing that she was being irrational but simply not caring. "You should have warned your men that it was poisonous to horses. You should have known!"

"That's enough, Mandy," Dr. Emily said, putting her hand on Mandy's arm. She turned to Sam Western. "I'm afraid that Matty has eaten some water hemlock roots."

Sam Western frowned. "Will she get better?"

"As if you care!" Mandy shook away her mom's hand, the words bursting from her. "You hate all animals!"

A pink flush spread over Sam Western's face. "Now, that's not true. I don't hate animals," he blustered.

"Yes, you do!" Mandy cried. "You always have! In fact," she gasped as she looked at poor Matty's prone body beside her, "you're probably *glad* that Matty's ill!" With that, she turned and ran up field.

Mandy didn't stop running until she reached the stable. Throwing herself down on a bale of hay, she gave way to her tears. "Oh, Matty!" she sobbed. "Please don't die!"

There was the sound of footsteps behind her.

"Mandy?" It was her mom's voice.

For a moment, Mandy didn't move. She knew her mom would be furious with her for being so rude, but she hadn't been able to stop herself. She continued to cry.

"Oh, Mandy," her mom said in a quieter voice and Mandy felt her sit down beside her and put a hand on her shoulder.

She looked up, her face streaked with tears. "I hate him, Mom," she sobbed.

Dr. Emily pulled her close and stroked her hair. "Matty being ill really isn't Sam Western's fault," she said softly. "He didn't know that there was cowbane in the ditches or that Matty would eat some before the men had a chance to clear it away."

Mandy sniffed. "He hates animals."

"He doesn't hate them, love. He just sees animals very differently from the way we do." Dr. Emily sighed. "But that certainly doesn't give you the right to speak to him like you did." Mandy glanced up at her. "You're going to have to apologize."

"No!" Mandy exclaimed, pulling back from her mom and staring at her in horror. "No, I won't!"

"Yes, you will," Dr. Emily said firmly.

"It's not fair!" she protested, but she knew deep down that her mom was right.

Her mom simply stood up and motioned toward the door.

Mandy walked reluctantly down the field. She saw James look at her anxiously but she didn't say anything

to him. Red in the face but holding her head high, she marched up to Sam Western. "I'm sorry," she muttered, trying to sound as if she meant it.

To Mandy's surprise, Sam Western looked almost embarrassed. "That's all right," he said awkwardly. He cleared his throat and looked at Dr. Emily who had crouched beside Matty again to check her breathing and heart rate. "How's the mare doing, Dr. Emily?"

"Well, she's not getting any worse," Dr. Emily said, looking slightly relieved. "We're just going to have to see what happens over the next few hours."

Sam Western turned to the men. "Clear the site and then take the rest of the afternoon off. I don't want you disturbing the horse. It will be better if we get out of your way," he said quickly to Dr. Emily and Wilfred. "But if there's anything you need," he cleared his throat again, "just let me know."

Mandy stared in surprise as Sam Western turned and strode toward his car. He had almost sounded as though he cared what happened to Matty. For a moment, she was too stunned to move but then she remembered something. "Mr. Western!" she called, jumping to her feet. "What about the cats?"

Sam Western stopped. For a moment he seemed to hesitate. "They can stay until Sunday," he said quickly.

"We'll clean out that caravan last." A more familiar frown crossed his face. "But if they're not out then . . ."

"They will be!" Mandy gasped, looking at James in astonishment. Sunday was almost a whole week away. She was sure they could tempt the mother cat out by then. "Thank you!"

Without another word, Sam Western strode to his car.

Mandy kneeled down beside James. "Did you hear that? He's given us until Sunday!"

"Guilty conscience," James muttered darkly.

Mandy stroked Matty's neck. The mare's breathing seemed slightly easier but her muscles still twitched. "Is there anything else we can do, Mom?" she asked anxiously.

Dr. Emily shook her head. "Not at the moment." She took her phone from her pocket. "I'll call the clinic and let Jean know where I am," she said. She walked away a few paces and punched in the number.

Mandy looked at Wilfred. The old man's face was furrowed as he stared down at Matty. Mandy moved closer to him and squeezed his gnarled hand. "She'll be all right, Wilfred," she said. "She'll get better."

Wilfred continued to watch the gray mare closely. "Thanks, Mandy," he said at last. He placed his hand gently on Matty's velvety nose. "I don't know what I'd do without my girl." He shook his head. "I remember the day she was born. A skinny little thing with really long legs. It was Rose who delivered her." He smiled at the memory. "She was always more Rose's horse than mine. It was Rose who broke her in and Rose who started her off in the riding school." A shadow crossed Wilfred's face. "Now Rose is gone and Matty's all that I have left. I know that she's getting on in years and that one day she'll die, but not yet, surely. . . ." His words trailed off as he looked at the gray mare.

Mandy didn't know what to say and, looking at James, she could tell that he felt the same. The worry on Wilfred's face was awful to see. She stroked Matty's neck, wishing that there was something more she could do.

The minutes slowly ticked by into hours. Matty didn't get any better but at the same time she didn't seem to be getting any worse. After a while, Mandy's mom went to Wilfred's cottage and made some lunch and coffee for them all. But the tray remained barely touched. No one felt like eating much when Matty was so ill.

Suddenly, James jumped to his feet. "I'll go and put some water in the caravan for the cats," he said. "Now that we've blocked the escape route, the mother cat will need us to provide her with food and water. Are you coming?" he asked Mandy.

Mandy shook her head. Although she understood

James's urge to do something rather than just sit around waiting, she couldn't bring herself to leave Matty's side. She watched James hurry away.

"We should check Matty's pulse again," Dr. Emily said.

"I'll do it," Mandy said quickly. She took the stethoscope from her mom and placed it just behind Matty's elbow, as she'd been shown before. Looking at her watch, she counted how many heartbeats she could hear in a minute. "Fifty," she said to her mom, as she took the stethoscope from her ears.

"That's good," her mom said. "It's almost within the normal range."

Mandy leaned forward and lifted Matty's lips. She remembered her mum saying that pale gums, like a rapid or weakened pulse, were an indicator of shock. "Her gums are better, too," she said, showing Matty's pink gums to her mom. "And I'm sure the spasms are fewer."

Dr. Emily patted Matty's damp neck. "Come on, girl. You can do it. You've just got to keep fighting."

James returned a few minutes later. "The cats are OK," he told them. "The mother's eaten all the cat food that was in the bowl and she seems a little calmer. I gave her some water, but we should remember to leave some more food for her tonight."

"So you've got until Sunday to get them out?" Dr. Emily asked.

Mandy nodded. "Do you think we'll be able to?"

"I think you've got a good chance," her mom replied. "Just take it slowly. Spend as much time with them as you can. With the mother being shut in, she will rely on you for food. Feed her several times a day and hopefully she should start to accept you and look forward to your visits. But don't let her out of the trailer. If you do, she may move the kittens again, or even take fright and abandon them."

"I still can't believe that Sam Western's given us more time," James said.

Mandy shivered. "I wonder what he'd have done with the cats if he'd taken them away today."

"Killed them probably," James said grimly. "You saw his face when he heard that the cats were trapped in the caravan. I bet he just thinks they're pests that need to be dealt with."

"Look!" Wilfred said suddenly.

Mandy, James, and Dr. Emily looked around. Matty had raised her head from the grass. With a struggle, she heaved herself from her side on to her stomach. The cats were instantly forgotten. "Matty!" Mandy gasped.

The gray mare looked around. Her muscles gave the

occasional tremble but Mandy could see that her eyes had lost their wide, staring look.

A relieved smile lit up Dr. Emily's face. "She's fought off the poison! She's going to pull through."

Mandy could hardly believe it. A wave of delight overwhelmed her and she flung her arms around James. For once, he didn't look embarrassed. "Matty's going to be OK!" he gasped, his glasses falling down his nose.

Mandy didn't think she had ever felt happier. "Wilfred!" she cried, swinging around. "Matty's going to make it!"

Wilfred was still kneeling by the mare. He placed a shaky hand on Matty's head. "Oh, Matty," he said, his voice cracking with emotion. "I don't know how I'd have coped if you hadn't pulled through."

Lifting her nostrils to Wilfred's hair, Matty blew gently, affection for her owner shining in her dark eyes.

Six

As soon as Dr. Emily was sure that Matty was on the mend, she set off for Animal Ark. "Call me if she shows any signs of a relapse," she told Wilfred, as he led Matty into her stable. "Otherwise I'll come and check on her after this afternoon's clinic." She smiled at Mandy and James. "I'll pick you up then. Take good care of Matty."

"As if we'd do anything else," Mandy said, putting her arms around Matty's neck and giving her a hug.

Wilfred wanted to stay in the stable with Matty, so Mandy and James busied themselves around the stable. They tidied and swept the feed storeroom and brushed the mare's rugs, stopping occasionally to go and check on the cats. The mother still looked unsettled and they decided that it would be best to wait until the next day to start their plan for taming her.

"She should have calmed down a bit by then," Mandy said. "I bet all the noise outside has upset her even more."

At the end of the day, Wilfred came out of Matty's stable. "You've done a great job," he said, looking around at the folded rugs, clean tack, and freshly swept floor. "Thank you."

"That's all right," Mandy said, smiling. "We're just glad to help."

James glanced at his watch. "We should feed the cats," he said. "Your mom will be back soon."

They filled a plastic scoop with the cat food that they had brought from Animal Ark and made their way to the caravan. The cat was lying down, feeding her kittens, but as soon as they walked in, she sprang to her feet and hissed warningly at them. The kittens meowed in protest at having their meal interrupted. Shuffling after her, they butted their heads underneath her belly, searching for her milk. The mother stayed absolutely still, her eyes riveted on Mandy and James.

Trying not to make any sudden movements in case he frightened her, James edged forward and poured the contents of the scoop into the empty bowl. "We'll have to try and clean this place up a little tomorrow," he said, wrinkling his nose at the heavy smell of cats in the air.

Mandy nodded. "We can bring some newspaper and cover the floor," she said. "Then we can clean it out each day." She checked the cat's water. It was still full. As she looked up, she met the cat's suspicious amber gaze. "You'll be all right here," Mandy said softly, wishing that the cat didn't look as if she disliked them so much. "We're your friends. We'll take care of you and your kittens." The cat drew back slightly, her ears flattening against the sides of her head. She looked like the last thing she wanted was for Mandy and James to be her friends.

A sudden shiver of foreboding ran down Mandy's spine. Standing there so warily, the cat looked completely wild. Were they really going to be able to tame her in so short a time?

Getting out of the Land Rover at Animal Ark that evening, after they'd dropped James off, Mandy felt her legs wobble with exhaustion. It had been a very long, action-packed day. So much had happened — the cats disappearing, Sam Western's threats, Matty being ill. Mandy rubbed a hand across her eyes. It seemed like a lifetime since they had set off that morning with such high hopes of catching the cats.

"Supper, then an early bed for you, Mandy Hope," her mom said, looking at her in concern.

Mandy nodded, too tired to argue. But as she reached the back door, she remembered something. "Dylan!" she exclaimed. "How is he?"

Her mom smiled. "There's been a slight improvement today," she replied. "He lifted his head for the first time."

Mandy immediately forgot her tiredness. "Can I see him?" she asked excitedly.

"Come on, then," her mom said. "Just for a few minutes."

They went to the residential unit. As Dr. Emily unlocked the door, Mandy heard a faint whimper. She glanced at her mom.

"Yes, that's him," Dr. Emily said.

Mandy hurried through the door. Dylan was still lying down but when he saw her, his ears pricked up and he slowly lifted his head. Mandy reached into the puppy's cage and he stretched his muzzle toward her. "You *are* looking better," Mandy said, greatly relieved to see him looking so much more alert.

"Now we just have to get him onto his feet," Dr. Emily said, leaning over Mandy's shoulder. "He still doesn't seem to want to stand. And I wish he looked happier, the poor little mite."

As Mandy rubbed Dylan under his ears, she remembered what she had thought the night before. "Maybe he's missing his owners."

Her mom nodded. "Maybe. We didn't want them to visit until he showed some signs of recovery, in case it overstimulated him. But now that he's looking a bit brighter, it might do him good to see them. I'll give them a call this evening and see if they can drop by tomorrow."

"Dad, have you got any more ideas about how James and I could tame the cat?" Mandy asked as she helped her dad clear up after supper. "We haven't had much luck with her so far."

Dr. Adam considered the question as he began to rinse the pans. "Well, obviously feeding her is important, and you should keep your body language as unthreatening as possible. That means no sudden movements, and make sure you speak in a low voice," he explained. "And don't look her directly in the eye or face her straight on. To a cat or dog, that's like giving a direct challenge. So keep your eyes lowered and turn your shoulders at an angle to her."

Mandy nodded. All her dad's advice made sense. She put away the pans and began to make a mental list of the things she and James would need the next day — dry cat food, a clean food bowl, newspapers for the floor.

Just then, her mom came back in from phoning Dylan's owners, Sam and Liz Butler. "The Butlers are coming to see Dylan tomorrow afternoon," she announced. "I spoke to Liz. She sounded as though she could hardly wait."

"Oh, good," Mandy said, pleased.

Her mom smiled. "Why don't you go to bed, love? You look exhausted."

Mandy nodded. Her eyelids felt very heavy. "Night," she said, going across to her mom and dad and kissing them.

"Night, love," her dad replied. "Sweet dreams."

When Mandy woke up the next morning, it seemed unusually light outside. She glanced at her bedside clock and saw that it was quarter past eight! She had overslept by an hour and a half.

She jumped out of bed and threw on some clothes, then ran downstairs. Her mom was just about to go into the clinic. "I'm sorry!" Mandy gasped. Normally, she was up in time to clean out the cages in the residential unit and help give the patients their medication.

"It's OK," Dr. Emily said. "I thought it best to let you sleep in. Simon and I have seen to the animals." She smiled. "And there's good news from Wilfred. He phoned ten minutes ago to say that Matty's had a good night and is looking much brighter."

Mandy felt a weight lift from her shoulders. "That's great!"

Dr. Emily expertly twisted her long red hair into a knot at the nape of her neck, securing it with a clip. "Now, why don't you have some breakfast and then come and give Simon a hand?" she suggested as she headed for the door.

Mandy quickly ate a piece of toast and honey, then ran through to the clinic. Simon had just finished mopping the floor. "That was good timing," he grinned, squeezing the mop out in the bucket.

"Sorry, I overslept," Mandy apologized.

"I'll forgive you," Simon said. "But only if you empty this bucket for me."

Mandy took the bucket of dirty water from him. "Slave driver!" she teased.

She was emptying the bucket outside when she saw a dark-haired man help Mrs. Austin get out of a blue van in the parking lot. The man then lifted out Mrs. Austin's spaniel, Archie, and put him down gently onto the ground.

Mandy went over. "Hello, Mrs. Austin," she said. "Has Archie come in for his X rays?" She stroked the dog's soft, floppy ears.

The elderly lady nodded. "I hope we're not too early."

"No, you're right on time," Mandy said. "Come in."

She got Simon, who gave Mrs. Austin a form to fill in, and then they took Archie through to the residential unit.

Mandy was pleased to see Dylan look up as they entered. She got a piece of sheepskin and put it in the cage next to the puppy. "There we are, Archie," she said, carefully lifting the dog into the cage and unclipping his leash.

Mrs. Austin reached out and stroked her dog's head

with a trembling hand. "Be a good boy," she whispered to him.

"We'll look after him," Simon said kindly. "Don't worry, Mrs. Austin. He's in safe hands."

The old lady nodded and then, with one last look at Archie, she left.

Seven

It had been a busy morning at Animal Ark, but it was just starting to quiet down when James arrived. "Are you ready?" he asked Mandy.

"Yep," she replied. She poked her head into her mom's consultation room. "Is it OK if I go to Wilfred's now?"

Her mom looked up from the insurance form she was filling in for a patient. "Fine. Tell him I'll come by later to check on Matty."

Mandy nodded and then she and James loaded their bikes with cat food, newspapers, and cleaning equipment, and set off for Wilfred's.

The February sun was shining down and white clouds

blew briskly across a forget-me-not blue sky. Mandy felt her spirits lift. On a day like this, she couldn't help but feel optimistic. Surely the cat would soon see that she and James meant her family no harm?

Wilfred was in Matty's stable when they arrived. "How's Matty?" Mandy asked quickly.

"See for yourself," Wilfred said, opening the door for her.

Matty was pulling at a hay net, but hearing the door open, she looked around, her ears pricked and her eyes bright.

"She looks a lot better," James said.

Mandy dumped the armload of cat things that she was carrying, then went and patted the mare. "Hello, girl," she said. Matty snuffled her hair affectionately.

"She's thanking you for helping her yesterday," Wilfred said.

Mandy laughed, but, in a way, it almost felt as if Wilfred was right.

"So, we'll feed the mother first," James said, as they left the stable and headed for the caravan, discussing their plans for taming the cat. "Then we'll wait a bit for her to settle down before we clean out the mess and put some newspaper down."

"Keeping the door shut so she can't escape," Mandy

added, "and keeping our bodies turned sideways to her so she doesn't feel threatened." She put her hand on the door of the trailer. "Are you ready?"

James nodded. Mandy opened the door and they slipped inside.

The kittens had obviously been playing in the middle of the floor but, at the sound of the door opening, they scampered over to their mother at the back of the caravan. Hiding behind her, they peeked out at Mandy and James with their big blue eyes. The mother cat arched her back warningly.

Being careful not to look directly at her, Mandy and James refilled the food bowl and the saucer of water and pushed them toward her. Then they sat down and waited to see what would happen.

At first, the mother cat stayed where she was, but they could tell by the way her whiskers twitched and her eyes flickered every now and then to the bowl that she was interested in the food. Finally, her hunger seemed to get the better of her. Keeping a wary eye on Mandy and James, she ran to the food and, crouching down beside it, began to eat.

The kittens came to investigate the food bowl. As always, the black one was first. "They're too young to eat solid food yet, aren't they?" James said in a low voice, as the kittens dipped their heads into the bowl, sniffed the food, and then stumbled away on their short, unsteady legs.

Mandy nodded. "Yes. Kittens normally start eating regular food when they're about five weeks old."

Uninterested in the food, the kittens started to play. They were still uncoordinated and, as they tried to bat each other with their front paws, they overbalanced and rolled onto the floor.

"The black one's the liveliest," Mandy said, watching the black kitten tussle with the male gray-and-white kitten and then spring away and bounce at the smaller female kitten who was sitting watching them play.

James grinned at the kittens' antics. "We should think of names for them," he said.

"You're right," Mandy agreed. "Any ideas?"

James studied the kittens. "Well, the two gray-and-white ones look like they've been climbing up a chimney," he said. "How about calling the female Smudge, and the male Sweep?"

Mandy nodded enthusiastically. She liked the names. "Yes, and the black one could be . . ."

"Sooty!" they both said at precisely the same time.

Mandy grinned. "That's settled then."

"Not yet," James said. "There's still the mother. We

need something to go with Sooty, Smudge, and Sweep." He frowned for a moment. "Smoke?" he suggested, admiring the mother's beautiful gray coat.

"Too much like Smoky," Mandy said, thinking of her grandma and grandad's young cat. "How about Ash?"

James shook his head. "Too boyish. What about Cinders?"

Mandy loved it. "Brilliant!" she exclaimed. "Cinders, Sooty, Smudge, and Sweep. You're a genius, James!"

"I know," James grinned. "It's hard, but I just can't help it."

Mandy hit him playfully. "Idiot!"

The sudden movement made Cinders look up quickly from her saucer of water. Mandy immediately froze. To her relief, Cinders didn't run off. She stared at them for a moment with enormous amber eyes and then lowered her head and licked up the last few drops.

"She doesn't seem quite so scared of us," Mandy whispered to James.

"I know," he said, as Cinders trotted back to her nest at the back of the caravan.

They waited until Cinders settled down and then began to clean the floor. Cinders watched them warily, but she didn't leave the nest. Soon the floor was clean and covered with a layer of newspaper. Mandy didn't want to disturb Cinders by going too near the nest, so she pushed a piece of paper across the floor until it was almost touching the kittens.

Cinders backed off with a suspicious hiss, but Sooty spotted the corner of the moving sheet of paper and sprang on it playfully. Sweep joined him. Together they tussled with the corner, their tiny claws scratching through the paper.

"Look at Smudge, watching," Mandy whispered.

Smudge was sitting in the nest, her eyes wide in alarm, but her head moved from side to side as she followed her brothers' movements. She was the quietest of the three kittens. She looked as if she wanted to join in but didn't quite dare to. Finally, however, she couldn't resist. With a high-pitched meow, she sprang at Sooty's waving tail.

"They're so adorable," Mandy said, as the three kittens tumbled over one another, scrunching up the clean paper. "They deserve really good homes after such a bad start in life."

An hour later, Mandy and James left the trailer and went to Matty's stable. Dr. Emily had arrived and was talking to Wilfred. "How are the cats this morning?" she asked as they came in.

"OK," Mandy said. "Though the mom's still really nervous around us. What about Matty?"

"She seems to be making a perfect recovery," Dr.

Emily said. "I was just telling Wilfred that she'll need to take it easy for a few days — so no riding this spring break, I'm afraid — but she can go out in the field as long as there are absolutely no more cowbane roots lying around."

"We'll check for you, Wilfred," James offered quickly. "Come on, Mandy."

Before Mandy followed, she remembered something that had been at the back of her mind all morning. "Mom, how's Archie?" she asked. "Have you found out what's wrong with him?"

"Dad was just X-raying him as I came out," her mom replied. Her eyes met Mandy's. "Remember, Archie's old, love. It may not be good news."

"I hope he *is* OK," Mandy said, thinking of Mrs. Austin's worried face.

"So do I," her mom said.

After waving her mom off, Mandy and James went down the field and began to scour the grass near the ditches for uprooted cowbane, but the workmen seemed to have cleaned up well.

"I still can't believe that Sam Western didn't warn the workmen about cowbane," Mandy said angrily. "He knew Matty was in the field."

"He might not have known that it was poisonous to

horses," James said, trying to be fair. "And he did offer to help when he found out that Matty was ill."

"He probably just didn't want to look bad in front of his men," Mandy said. "You know he doesn't care about animals one bit." She shivered. "Just imagine what he'd do if he got his hands on Cinders and her kittens."

James nodded. "Yeah, I know." He frowned. "I hope they end up with people who will love them and look after them properly."

Mandy agreed. "I wish I could have one," she said longingly. But it was impossible. Life at Animal Ark was just too busy.

"Me, too," James said. "But Mom and Dad would never agree. They think that Blackie and Eric are enough." Eric, James's young cat, had himself been part of another litter of kittens that they had rescued.

"Oh, well," Mandy went on, determined not to look on the downside. "It's too soon to be thinking about permanent homes for them. We have to get them out of the caravan first."

Mandy and James spent most of the day in the trailer. But even though Cinders appeared to be slightly more relaxed with them, she still seemed determined not to let them anywhere near her. Whenever they tried to approach her, she arched her back and spat warn-ingly.

"Maybe she'll be better tomorrow," James said hope-fully, as they walked up the field that afternoon.

Mandy sighed. "Maybe."

"We could buy some treats and try tempting her with them," James suggested.

Mandy liked the idea. "OK," she said. "Let's buy some at the store tomorrow."

After saying good-bye to Wilfred, they biked back into the village."

"I'd better go and walk Blackie," James said, stopping his bike at the village green. "He can't understand why he's not allowed to come with me each day, but I don't want to risk him frightening the cats."

"See you tomorrow," Mandy said. Then she went on to Animal Ark.

As she swung into the drive, her feet suddenly slowed on the pedals and she skidded to a stop. Her mom was helping Mrs. Austin into the same blue van that Mandy had seen that morning. Mrs. Austin was clutching a col-lar and leash and looked as if she was crying.

Mandy suddenly felt sick. Where was Archie? Drop-ping her bike on the ground, she ran over to her mom, who was watching the van pull away. "Mom!" Mandy gasped. "What's happened to Archie?"

Dr. Emily looked at her sadly and took her hand. "He's been put to sleep, love."

"Why?" Mandy gasped.

"The X rays showed that he had an advanced bone tumor," her mom explained quietly. "It was inoperable and he was in pain. When Mrs. Austin came in, she decided that the kindest thing was to put Archie to sleep before he suffered any more."

For a moment, Mandy couldn't speak. She knew that it was impossible to cure every animal who came into Animal Ark, but it didn't make it any easier when an animal was put to sleep.

Her mom seemed to understand how she was feeling. "It was for the best, love. He'd had a long and happy life, and it wouldn't have been fair to let him suffer."

Mandy knew she was right but it still seemed so unfair. "Will . . . will Mrs. Austin get another dog?" she asked.

"I don't think so," her mom said. "I asked her and she said that she didn't think she could bear to have one after having Archie for so long."

Just then, Jean Knox put her head out of the door. "There's a phone call for you, Emily."

"OK, I'm coming," Dr. Emily called back. She looked at Mandy. "It's been very hectic this afternoon. Can you come and help?" she asked.

Mandy guessed that her mom wanted to keep her

busy so that she wouldn't think about Archie too much. "OK," she said.

She put her bike away and went into the clinic. As usual, there was lots to do and, as she threw herself into the work, she found that the familiar tasks did provide some sort of comfort.

Just as the clinic was finishing, Sam and Liz Butler, Dylan's owners, arrived. They looked pale and anxious.

"We've come to see Dylan," Liz said to Jean Knox. "Dr. Emily called us last night."

"I'll get her," Jean said.

As Jean went to find Dr. Emily, Mandy entered the residential unit to check on Dylan. The puppy was lying sadly on his blanket. She opened the door of the cage and stroked his soft head. "You've got visitors, boy," she said. "Cheer up."

But Dylan just stared at her with mournful brown eyes.

Dr. Emily led Mr. and Mrs. Butler through to the residential unit.

"How is he?" Mandy heard Sam Butler say.

In his cage, Dylan started and pricked his ears. Mandy stood back so that he could see his owners.

"He's improving slightly," Dr. Emily said, opening the door to the unit. "But he's still very quiet."

"Dylan?" Liz Butler said, coming in cautiously. Mandy

saw her eyes widen as she took in the stitches and swollen skin along her puppy's shaved neck. "Oh, Dylan!" She rushed up to the cage.

For a moment, Dylan stared as if he couldn't believe what he was seeing. Then with a high-pitched whimper of delight, he stretched out his front paws.

"Mom! Look!" Mandy gasped, as the puppy scrambled unsteadily to his feet.

Sam Butler came and stood beside his wife. "Hello, boy," he said.

With another whimper, Dylan stumbled toward them. His back legs almost seemed to give way, but with an enormous effort he managed to stay on his feet. Reaching Liz and Sam, he began to lick them ecstatically.

Tears of happiness sprang to Mandy's eyes.

"I think you were right, Mandy," her mom said softly, coming over and putting an arm around her shoulders. "This was just the medicine that Dylan needed."

Looking at the joy on the Butlers' faces and at Dylan's frantically wagging tail, Mandy knew that there was nothing she wanted more in the world than to be a vet, like her mom and dad.

Eight

The next morning, Mandy told James all about Dylan as they biked to the store to buy some treats for Cinders.

"He's going home this afternoon," she told him. "Liz and Sam, his owners, are going to take some time off work to look after him."

"That's great!" James said, stopping his bike outside the store.

Mandy nodded. "I know. I'll miss him, but I'm just really glad he's going to get better."

The doorbell tinkled as they walked in. The general store seemed to sell just about everything anyone could want to buy. Mrs. McFarlane was tidying the shelves. "Hello, you two," she said with her usual ready smile. "What can I get you today?"

"Some cat treats, please, Mrs. McFarlane," James replied.

Mrs. McFarlane wiped her hands on her gaily striped apron and climbed up her stepladder. "Are they for Eric?" she asked, taking down a box of treats.

James shook his head. "They're for a stray cat we've found. We're trying to tame her," he said.

"The cat and her three kittens are living in one of the caravans on Sam Western's campsite," Mandy explained. "Sam Western won't let them stay there, so we want to take them somewhere safe. But we have to win the mother cat's trust, first."

Mrs. McFarlane shook her head. "I sometimes wonder what the animals around Welford would do without the pair of you." She handed the treats to James. "Go on, you can have them for nothing," she said, seeing him dig in his pockets for some money. "It's for a good cause."

"Oh, thanks, Mrs. McFarlane!" James exclaimed.

Just then, Ernie Bell came in. Ernie had lived in the village all his life and he was good friends with Mandy's grandfather. He nodded at Mandy and James. "Morning," he said shortly.

"Hi, Ernie," Mandy said cheerfully. She knew better than to be put off by Ernie's gruff exterior. He had often helped her and James in the past — building fences, releasing rabbits into the wild, and even adopting a squirrel.

"Mandy and James were just telling me about a stray cat they've been trying to catch," Mrs. McFarlane said, eager as usual to pass on village news. "Up at Sam Western's campsite. In one of his trailers."

Ernie raised his eyebrows. "In one of the trailers? I bet young Sam Western isn't too happy about that," he said.

"No, he isn't. That's why we're trying to move her," Mandy explained.

She and James stepped away from the counter as Ernie bought his morning paper and then followed him outside into the warm sunshine.

"Mrs. McFarlane's just given us these," James said, holding out the foil-wrapped treats for Ernie to see. "We thought we could tempt her near us."

Ernie peered at them. "Salmon-flavored," he read from the packet. He sniffed scornfully. "You don't need new-fangled things like that. All you need is a little catnip."

"Catnip?" Mandy echoed. She knew that catnip was a green herb that lots of cats loved to sniff and play in.

"Yup, catnip," Ernie said. "You mark my words, take

some into this trailer with you and that cat will soon be rolling over and playing like a kitten."

"Well, we could try it as well. Where can we get some?" Mandy asked.

"Try your grandad, girl. He's bound to have some in that garden of his."

Mandy was sure that Ernie was right. Her grandad was a very good gardener and grew all sorts of herbs, vegetables, and flowers in his garden. "OK, we will," she said, looking at James, who nodded.

They said good-bye to Ernie and biked around to Lilac Cottage, where Mandy's grandparents lived. Snowdrops nodded in terracotta pots around the door. Mandy rapped on the knocker.

A few moments later, her grandma opened the door. She was wearing a bright turquoise tracksuit. "Mandy! James!" she said, her face breaking into a broad smile. "What a nice surprise. You should have told me you were coming. I was just off to the village hall to play badminton with Margaret Davy."

"It's OK, Grandma," Mandy said, kissing her. "We're not going to stay for long. Is Grandpa here?"

Grandma looked over her shoulder. "Tom!" she called. "Mandy and James want to see you. Come into the kitchen," she said to them. "He'll be through in a minute."

They followed her into the cozy kitchen. "Now sit down," said Grandma, opening her cookie jar. "And have a cookie. Ginger ones — baked yesterday."

Mandy and James helped themselves from the jar. "Thanks, Grandma," Mandy said. "These look delicious."

Her grandma looked pleased. "So, what do you want with your grandpa?" she asked, sitting down opposite them.

Before Mandy could reply, her grandpa came through to the kitchen. He smiled when he saw them. "Good morning, you two," he said cheerfully. "What can I do for you?"

Mandy and James quickly explained about Cinders and her kittens and about meeting Ernie in the store. "He said we should try taking some catnip into the caravan," Mandy said, through a mouthful of cookie. "And so we were wondering if you had any."

Grandpa Hope nodded. "I've got several clumps of it," he said. "The bees love it in the summer. If you come into the garden, I'll cut you some."

"Great!" said Mandy, hastily finishing her cookie. "Come on, James!"

"I'll see you soon," Grandma called from the doorway as Mandy and James followed Grandpa into the garden.

"I've got to dash or Margaret will think I've forgotten her."

"Bye!" Mandy waved as her grandma set off with her sports bag in one hand and her badminton racket in the other. Sometimes Mandy wondered if her grandma had ever heard the term "a quiet retirement." If she wasn't playing badminton or sitting on committees, she was baking cakes for the Women's Institute or setting out on yet another holiday with Grandpa in their camper van.

"Here we are," Grandpa said, stopping by a low green bush. "Catnip, otherwise known as *Nepeta cataria*."

"It looks like mint," James said, looking at the small, veined leaves.

"That's because it is a member of the mint family," Grandpa Hope agreed. He picked off a couple of leaves and handed them to Mandy and James to smell. "Now, if you wait here, I'll get some pruning shears."

Mandy and James soon had a plastic bag full of catnip cuttings. "Thanks, Grandpa," Mandy said, as they picked up their bikes.

"Anytime," Grandpa Hope smiled. "I just hope it does the trick. Not all cats love catnip, you know. Some of them go wild for it, but others don't seem to have the slightest interest. I asked your dad about it once and he said that some cats are simply born unable to detect the smell."

"I hope Cinders can smell it," James said to Mandy.
"Me, too," she agreed.

"Cinders will be ready for her breakfast," Mandy said
when she and James finally reached the campsite. "It's
very late."

They got a scoop of dry food and some fresh newspapers from the supplies they had left in the feed room
and walked over to the caravan, which looked cozy and
cheerful in the bright morning sun.

The cats were in their nest. Cinders stood up as they
entered. But this time she didn't shrink back. She stood
her ground, her amber eyes flickering to the scoop that
James was carrying. He started to pour the food into
the empty bowl.

"Look!" Mandy whispered. James glanced up. Cinders was creeping toward him, her eyes fixed on the dry
food. She stopped warily a couple of yards away.

Very quietly, James stepped back a pace. It was enough
to give Cinders confidence. Bounding forward, she began
to gobble down the food in big hungry mouthfuls.

"She's definitely getting tamer," James whispered.

Mandy nodded, hope brimming up inside her. Maybe
this would be the day that they got Cinders and her family out of the trailer.

While Cinders ate, Sooty and Sweep came over to investigate Mandy and James. Sweep pounced on Mandy's hand, clawing at it and overbalancing. She laughed and tickled his fluffy white tummy. "Come on, Smudge," she said, seeing the other gray-and-white kitten sitting a little way off, watching. "Come and play." Mandy wriggled her fingers invitingly on the floor.

Smudge hesitated for a moment and then plucked up her courage and trotted over.

"They're so cute!" James said, picking Sooty up and letting the lively black kitten claw all the way up his sweater to his shoulder.

It didn't take long for Cinders to finish her food. She went back to the nest, stretched, and then lay down. The kittens immediately bounded over, and, snuggling underneath her, they began to feed.

Moving quietly so as not to disturb them, Mandy and James removed the dirty papers and replaced them with clean sheets. "That's better," Mandy said at last, looking around the caravan with a feeling of satisfaction. She nudged James. "Look." Full of milk, the kittens had curled up together and gone to sleep.

"We could bring the treats and the catnip in," James suggested, "and see if we can get Cinders to come close to us while the kittens are sleeping. She's looking pretty relaxed."

Mandy nodded and fetched the bag from outside. As

she opened it, the minty smell of the freshly cut catnip filled the caravan.

"Mmm, it smells delicious," James said, sniffing.

"Let's hope Cinders thinks so, too," Mandy said, glancing at the gray cat.

"She *looks* interested," James said. Cinders had sat up and was staring at them. "Let's put some on the floor and see what she does."

Taking the catnip out of the bag, they spread it out on the floor. Then they sat down nearby to watch.

Cinders's whiskers twitched as she breathed in the sweet scent of the herb. Suddenly, she opened her mouth and curled back her upper lip.

"Eric does that sometimes," James whispered, remembering his own cat reacting in the same way.

"Yes, I've seen him," Mandy whispered back. "Dad told me that cats do it when they smell something interesting. They trap the smell on their tongue and then press their tongue against the roof of their mouth. It's like a cross between tasting and smelling."

"She's coming over," James said.

They both held their breath as Cinders edged across the floor toward the catnip. She stopped every few seconds to glance at Mandy and James, but because neither of them moved she seemed to gain courage. Reaching the catnip, she lowered her head and sniffed delicately at the minty leaves. It was the closest she had ever been to them, but she seemed too intrigued by the catnip to care.

Mandy watched, entranced, as Cinders chewed one of the leaves and then crouched down and rubbed her head against the stalks. Suddenly, the little cat threw herself down on the ground and rolled over and over. Jumping to her feet, she meowed excitedly.

It was the first time Mandy had seen Cinders look so playful and relaxed. With her amber eyes alight, she looked almost like a kitten again. Mandy was even more determined that Cinders should have a good home — a home where she would be loved and cared for to make up for the hard start she'd had in life.

"Do you think we can get closer to her?" James whispered eagerly.

Mandy looked at Cinders, who was sniffing the leaves again. "I'll try," she replied.

She waited until Cinders looked relaxed and then she leaned forward. The gray cat was so close that she could almost touch her. Holding her breath, Mandy reached out. For one moment, her fingers hovered over Cinder's back but suddenly the little cat noticed how near she was. Cinders froze and then, leaping into the air, she fled to the back of the caravan.

"Oh!" Mandy exclaimed in frustration.

"You were so close," James groaned.

Mandy pushed a hand through her hair. "Now what do we do?" She looked at Cinders who was crouching in the corner, staring at them with fear in her eyes.

"Try some treats?" James suggested.

Eager to try anything that might get them close to Cinders again, Mandy opened the packet of salmon-flavored treats and scattered a few around the food bowl and over the floor in front of them.

"OK, let's see what happens," she said.

They sat back down and waited. Cinders's whiskers trembled as she smelled the treats. But her courage was gone and she made no move toward them.

"It's no good," Mandy said, after twenty minutes had passed. "She's not going to come near us now. I shouldn't have tried to touch her. We're going to have to take things more slowly."

James looked anxious. "But time's running out, Mandy. Sam Western's coming in three days. We *have* to tame her by then."

A shiver of worry crept down Mandy's spine. Three days! Was that all? "We'll do it," she said resolutely. "We just have to keep on trying."

However, Cinders kept a wary distance for the rest of the day. Thursday slipped into Friday, and Friday into

Saturday. Each day, Cinders came a little closer to them but as soon as Mandy or James showed any sign of touching her, she panicked and fled.

"We're not getting anywhere," James groaned on Saturday morning, as they watched Cinders make her now-familiar dash back to the nest.

"She *is* getting better," Mandy insisted. "She just took a treat from my hand."

"Yeah, and then she ran away," James said. "What are we going to do? Sam Western's coming tomorrow."

Mandy took a deep breath. She hated to admit it, but she was running out of ideas. "If only we had more time," she said.

Seemingly unaware of their mother's fear, the three kittens were milling playfully around her feet. "At least *they're* tame," Mandy said, picking Sweep up and giving him a cuddle. "They'd come out of the caravan with us right now, wouldn't you?" she added to the kitten.

As she spoke, Sooty pounced on her sneaker laces and began to bat them with his front paws. Mandy smiled. Over the past week, all three kittens had become increasingly coordinated. They could now pounce without falling over and, instead of staggering around the trailer with their heads low, they trotted, with their tails held up, looking very sweet.

Mandy put Sweep down, and the two kittens began to wrestle with each other. As well as becoming more co-ordinated, they had just started to pick at their mother's food. In another few weeks Cinders would start to wean them, and then they would be ready to go to new homes.

Mandy bit her lip. But first she and James had to get Cinders out of the caravan. The kittens were too young to survive without her. And even if they were older, Mandy knew there was no way she could leave Cinders in the trailer for Sam Western to deal with. No, it was up to her and James to rescue the whole family of cats. But how?

James seemed to be wondering the same thing. "Maybe we're just going to have to catch her by force," he said. "Put a blanket over her like we were going to before and bundle her into the carrier. At least then we'd get her out."

"But she'd never trust us again," Mandy objected. She hated the idea of using force. Cinders's trust in them had grown over the last week and Mandy was afraid that if they destroyed that trust now, then taming her a second time might prove impossible.

"So what other ideas have you got?" James asked.

Mandy sighed. "None," she admitted. "But we've still got all of today and this evening."

Just then, they heard the noise of a car engine outside. "I wonder who that is?" James said in surprise.

They went to the door and looked out. Sam Western's Land Rover was bouncing over the grass toward the caravans.

"What're *they* doing here?" Mandy said as it stopped and Sam Western and Dennis Saville got out.

Dennis Saville opened the back door and let out Sam Western's two bulldogs. Fear suddenly shot through Mandy. "James!" she gasped. "Maybe they've come for Cinders and the kittens!"

"They can't have. Sam Western said he wouldn't come till tomorrow," James said quickly. But Mandy saw that his face had gone pale.

Sam Western and Dennis Saville marched toward them. The bulldogs pulled on their leashes beside them, panting and straining with every step.

Mandy bounded down the steps, her heart pounding. "Why are you here?" she exclaimed as the two men drew closer.

Sam Western stopped. His eyebrows rose superciliously. "Why am *I* here?" he queried. "I happen to own this land, in case you'd forgotten."

"We've come to see if those cats are still in that caravan," Dennis Saville snapped.

"Yes, they are," Mandy said, her mouth going dry. See-

ing the menace in Dennis Saville's hard eyes, she took a step backward. "But you can't take them!"

Dennis Saville ignored her. "I told you they'd still be here," he growled to his employer. His grip tightened on the dogs' leashes. "Shall I get them out for you, Mr. Western?"

"No!" Mandy exclaimed. The dogs snarled and barked but she ignored them. "You promised we could have till tomorrow!" she appealed to Sam Western.

"I'm going to be busy tomorrow," he replied firmly. "You can have until six o'clock this evening."

"But that's not fair!" Mandy exclaimed.

"It's only a few hours' difference," Sam Western said. He turned to Dennis Saville. "Call Andrew Austin and tell him to meet us here tonight. It looks like he's going to have to deal with them after all." Turning on his heel, he marched away.

Mandy saw a look of disappointment cross Dennis Saville's face. It was clear that he would have liked nothing better than to deal with the cats then and there, but he obviously knew better than to argue with his boss. With one last look at the trailer door, he followed Sam Western back up the field.

Mandy watched until the two men got back into the Land Rover. As it drove away, her legs felt suddenly wobbly and she sank down on the caravan steps. "They're coming back tonight," she said.

"I know," James said in a shaky voice. He glanced at the caravan door. "Mandy, what are we going to do?"

"We've got to get Cinders and the kittens out," Mandy said. "Come on, James. There's no time to lose!"

Nine

Mandy and James took the pet carriers into the caravan and tried tempting Cinder with cat food and treats, but the more they tried, the more nervous she seemed to become. She shot away from them every time.

"Please, Cinders," Mandy begged. "You've really got to let us catch you."

But Cinders took no notice.

They had just reached the point of despair when there was a knock at the caravan door. Mandy froze and looked at James.

"It isn't . . ." Mandy whispered, her heart clenching.

James seemed to read her mind. "Sam Western wouldn't knock," he said quickly.

Realizing he was right, Mandy hurried to the door. She was relieved to see it was just Wilfred.

"Your mom's been on the phone," he said. "She wanted to know if you were all right. She seemed surprised when I said you were still here."

Mandy glanced at her watch. It was almost four-thirty! It was no wonder her mom was wondering where she was.

Wilfred seemed to notice her pale face. "Is everything all right?" he asked in concern.

"No," Mandy said desperately. "Sam Western's coming to get the cats tonight!"

"Tonight?" Wilfred echoed.

Mandy nodded. "Can I call Mom from your house, Wilfred. I have to tell her what's happening."

"Of course, Mandy," Wilfred said.

Mandy ran up to the cottage and rang Animal Ark. She quickly told her mom about Sam Western's visit. "He's coming back at six o'clock," she said desperately. "And we can't catch Cinders."

Her mom immediately understood. "Keep trying. I'll come up as soon as I can and see what I can do," she promised. "And Betty Hilder called. She's back from her vacation and her assistant told her you had found some feral cats. Betty said she's very happy to look after them at the animal sanctuary."

"Thank goodness!" Mandy gasped. "At least we have somewhere safe to take Cinders and her kittens."

"Now keep calm," Dr. Emily told her. "If you're tense, Cinders will pick up on that and be even more frightened."

Mandy put the phone down just as Wilfred came into the cottage.

"Mom's coming," she told him.

Wilfred opened the fridge. "Here," he said, reaching in and handing her a plate with a whole cooked chicken on it. "Maybe the cat will come for this."

Mandy shook her head. "Thanks, Wilfred," she said. "It's very kind of you but we can't take it." She knew that Wilfred didn't have much money and that the chicken was probably his supper and lunch for the next few days.

"Of course you can," he said, starting to cut it up into pieces.

Mandy hesitated for a moment. Wilfred's chin was set and it was clear he wasn't going to take no for an answer. Quickly deciding that she would bring him something to make up for it the next day, she took the plate gratefully.

Wilfred smiled. "Just get those cats out before Sam Western comes back."

Mandy raced down the field with the chicken. She kept thinking about her mom's words. *Keep calm*, she told herself.

She found James in the caravan trying to tempt Cinders with a salmon-flavored treat. He had the two carriers open and ready, but the gray cat was just watching him warily from the nest. "What's that?" he asked, looking at the plate in Mandy's hand.

"It's chicken to tempt Cinders with," Mandy said. "Wilfred gave it to me." She took a deep breath. "Let's hope it works."

She crouched down and lowered the plate. As the smell of the chicken wafted into the air, the kittens, who had been playing in a corner, came trotting over confidently. Mandy offered them a tiny piece each. They smelled the tidbits and then pawed at her knee playfully.

"Look," James whispered.

The smell of the chicken had reached Cinders. Her whiskers quivered. Then, slowly, she began to creep toward them.

Handing the plate to James, Mandy took some chicken and held it out. "That's it, girl," she murmured. "We're not going to hurt you. . . ."

The cat crept closer until she was near enough to grab the chicken. This time, she didn't run straight off. She crouched down and ate it nearby.

While James tried to keep the meowing kittens away from the plate, Mandy offered Cinders another piece.

Cinders hardly hesitated. She took the chicken, swallowed it in one quick mouthful and then, to Mandy's amazement, stepped elegantly with one front paw onto Mandy's knees and tried to reach the plate that James was holding up.

Hardly daring to breathe, Mandy reached out and very gently touched Cinders's fur. The cat didn't seem to mind.

James glanced at her and Mandy saw he looked as delighted as she felt. Neither of them dared speak. James offered Cinders another piece of chicken. And then another, as paw by paw, the cat moved forward until she was balancing on all four paws on Mandy's lap.

Mandy's heart was racing with excitement at having Cinders so close. She forced herself to keep calm. She mustn't wreck things now. "There's a good girl," she whispered.

As she spoke, Cinders's eyes met hers. For one heart-stopping moment, Mandy thought that the little cat was about to turn and run. But then the last glimmer of fear seemed to leave Cinders's amber eyes. Stretching her head out, she rubbed against Mandy's sleeve and purred.

It was the moment Mandy had been hoping for all week. Feeling as if she was in a dream, she stroked the cat. Cinders arched her back against Mandy's hand and purred again. Very gently, Mandy took Cinders in her arms and stood up. Suddenly, she was sure that trying to put Cinders in the carrier would only frighten her and maybe make her panic. Mandy knew that she would have to carry her out.

"I'll bring the kittens," James said, realizing what Mandy was going to do. He scooped the three kittens up and put them into one of the carriers.

"Don't close the lid," Mandy said, as she felt Cinders look around to see what was happening to her babies. "Bring them like that."

Nodding, James picked the carrier up, ready to follow Mandy.

Mandy could hardly breathe, she was so excited. They were going to do it. They were actually going to get the cats out! Cuddling Cinders close, she pushed open the door and walked down the steps.

Suddenly, she stopped. Sam Western's familiar Land

Rover and a dark blue van were drawing up by the campsite entrance.

"Looks like we got Cinders out just in time," James said, stopping beside Mandy. They watched as a tall, burly man in overalls, carrying a cat carrier and a long metal stick with a hoop at one end, got out of the van and joined Sam Western by the Land Rover.

Mandy's legs felt shaky with relief as she looked at the metal stick in the man's hands. Sam Western was too late. The cats were safe!

The two men came striding across the grass. Suddenly, Sam Western seemed to notice Mandy and James. "The cats!" he exclaimed, stopping in front of them. "You got them out."

"Yes," Mandy replied triumphantly.

Just then, Sooty seemed to decide that he was bored with the cardboard carrier and he began to struggle out of it, his paws clawing as his head poked over the top of the box.

Mandy saw Sam Western turn pale. "Keep it away from me!" he ordered.

Mandy frowned. The big man looked almost afraid of Sooty. "He's only a kitten," she said, as James expertly captured Sooty and pushed him down into the box.

"I don't care," Sam Western said coldly. "I don't want any of them near me."

Mandy glared at him. "Well, you don't have to worry about that. We're taking them away. You won't ever have them near you again. Come on, James."

They started to march past when suddenly the man with the metal pole spoke. "I thought they were wild," he said, looking puzzled.

Mandy stopped. The man's deep voice sounded unexpectedly warm. "They were," Mandy agreed, holding Cinders close to her chest. "But we've tamed them."

"Well done," the man said. He held up the pole. "I

hate using this, but with wild cats it's often the only way."

Mandy looked at him warily but he seemed friendly. In fact, she realized, he also seemed quite familiar. She was sure she had seen him before.

"So, have you got homes for them?" the man asked next.

"Oh, yes," said Mandy. At least, Betty Hilder would take good care of Cinders and her family until proper homes were found for them.

"That's a pity." The man took off his gloves and, to Mandy's amazement, he bent down to tickle Sooty's black fluffy head. "I could have offered them a good home."

Mandy and James exchanged astonished looks.

"My mother had her old dog put down this week," the man went on. "It really upset her and she says she won't have another dog. But I'm worried about her getting lonely. When Mr. Western told me about the cats, I thought they'd be ideal. I hoped that a family of stray cats who need lots of love and attention might be just the thing to help my mom get over Archie's death — Archie was her dog," he explained.

"Archie!" Mandy stared at him, everything clicking into place as she realized why his face seemed so familiar. He was the man she had seen dropping Mrs. Austin off at Animal Ark. "Is your mom Mrs. Austin?"

It was the man's turn to look surprised. "That's right," he replied. "Do you know her?"

"I'm Mandy Hope. My mom and dad are the vets at Animal Ark," Mandy babbled. "I saw her and Archie there."

"You saw how upset she was then," the man said. "It's nice to meet you, Mandy. My name's Andrew." He looked at Cinders and the kittens. "Well, it's a pity, but if you've already got homes lined up. . . ."

"But we haven't," Mandy burst out. "Not really. We were just going to take them to the animal sanctuary. But if you want them for your mom then you can have them." She looked at James who nodded quickly.

"We didn't really want to take them to the sanctuary," James said. "It was just that they couldn't stay here. It would be great if the family could all stay together."

"So I can have them?" Andrew Austin asked.

"Yes!" Mandy and James said together.

A broad smile broke out on Andrew Austin's face. "That's wonderful."

Sam Western cleared his throat behind them. "Well, I'm glad you haven't had a wasted journey, Andrew."

Mandy realized that she had almost forgotten that Sam Western was there. It seemed almost impossible that he had arranged for someone as nice as Andrew to come and get the cats. "You didn't tell us that you were going to have the cats rehomed," she said to him.

"I said I would deal with them," Sam Western replied. "What did you think I meant?"

"That . . . that you'd shoot them or something," Mandy replied, feeling rather uncomfortable.

"Shoot them!" Sam Western looked genuinely astonished. "Why would I do that? I might not want a cat as a pet but I know they're useful. They keep down rats and mice. In fact, that's why I called Andrew. I thought he might have space for them on the farm."

"I manage Mr. Western's new organic farm," Andrew explained to Mandy and James. "When he found some cats here a few months ago I took them off his hands, so he thought that I might take this litter as well. But I've got enough cats now, so I thought about my mom."

Mandy could hardly believe what she was hearing. "But I thought you hated cats," she said to Sam Western.

The burly landowner eyed Cinders and her kittens warily. "I don't hate them, but I certainly don't like them," he admitted. "I was badly scratched by one when I was little and I've had a phobia about them ever since, but I wouldn't want to kill them. They're not pests like foxes or rabbits."

Mandy felt her hackles rise at the way Sam Western

talked about foxes and rabbits, but she bit back the angry words that sprang to her tongue. She had very different views on wild animals, but even she had to admit that she had judged him a bit too harshly when it came to cats.

Andrew reached into the carrier and stroked the three kittens. "Well, I guess we had better put these little things in the van then," he said. He looked at Cinders in Mandy's arms. "Will she go in a carrier?"

"I'm not sure," Mandy said. "She's been very nervous up to now and I don't think she'll react well to being shut up."

Andrew scratched his beard. "Hmm. Well, I can't drive with her loose in the van," he said. "It wouldn't be safe." He frowned thoughtfully. "But I don't want to frighten her."

"We could come with you," James suggested.

Mandy nodded. "That way we could hold them and they wouldn't be a nuisance."

"Are you sure?" Andrew asked. "I can bring you back afterward, but won't your parents mind?"

"We could call them from Wilfred's," Mandy said. However, just as she spoke, her mom's Land Rover drove into the campsite. Mandy grinned. "In fact, I can ask Mom right now." She carried Cinders carefully over to her mother, who was climbing out of the Land Rover.

Dr. Emily looked very surprised and relieved. "So you caught her?" she said.

"Yes, and that's not all," Mandy replied, her eyes shining. "We've found a home for them — a really wonderful home!"

Soon it was all settled. When she heard the story, Dr. Emily offered to give Mandy, James, and the cats a lift to Mrs. Austin's house so that Andrew didn't have to make an unnecessary journey to bring Mandy and James home.

"I can't wait to see Mrs. Austin's face," James said, as he and Mandy climbed into the Land Rover.

"I hope she's pleased," Mandy said. Andrew had told them that he hadn't said anything to his mother about the cats in case something had gone wrong. It was going to be a complete surprise for the old lady.

They set off, following Andrew's van. As they drove through the gathering dusk, Mandy and James filled Mandy's mom in on all the details.

"So Sam Western wasn't being quite so awful as you thought," Dr. Emily said, shooting an amused look at Mandy.

"No," Mandy said grudgingly. "But I still don't like him."

"Me, neither," James agreed.

"Well, somehow I don't think that's ever going to change," Dr. Emily said. "You both see animals as individuals with thoughts and feelings, whereas Mr. Western simply splits them into two groups: those that are useful to him and those that are pests." She glanced over her shoulder and smiled at them. "For my money, I think the world would be a much better place if more people thought the way you two do. I'm very proud of you."

Mandy felt her cheeks go pink and she buried her face in Cinder's soft fur. "I hope Mrs. Austin likes you, Cinders," she said, changing the subject.

"I think we're about to find out," her mom remarked.

They had reached Twyford village. Andrew pulled up outside a row of pretty stone cottages.

"Well," said Dr. Emily, parking behind him. "I guess it's time to see what Mrs. Austin's going to make of her new companions."

Mandy climbed out of the Land Rover with James, both carefully holding the cat family. They hung back, feeling slightly awkward, as Andrew knocked on one of the cottage doors. Mandy held Cinders close. What would Mrs. Austin say? Suddenly, she felt a little nervous. What if Mrs. Austin didn't want Cinders and the kittens?

The cottage door opened and Mrs. Austin looked out. "Andrew? What are you doing here?" she asked, the lines of her face deepening with confusion.

"I've brought you a little surprise." Her son grinned at her. "Mandy, James," he said, beckoning to them.

"You're the girl from the vet's!" Mrs. Austin exclaimed,

looking even more bewildered as Mandy stepped forward with James.

"Now, I know you said that you didn't want another dog after Archie," Andrew began, "so I thought that a cat and three kittens might do instead."

"Oh!" Mrs. Austin's hand flew to her mouth as she stared at Cinders in Mandy's arms. "Oh, Andrew, no, I really don't want a pet, not again."

Mandy's heart sank as Mrs. Austin shook her head and stepped backward. But just then, Sooty gave a high-pitched meow and poked his head out of the top of the carrier. He looked around, his fluffy fur sticking straight up.

"Oh," Mrs. Austin said, stopping dead in her tracks, her tone changing. "But he's adorable."

"They *all* are," Andrew said with a smile. As if on cue, Sweep and Smudge popped their gray-and-white heads over the top of the carrier on either side of Sooty's, and gazed around with wide, blue eyes.

"Just *look* at them," Mrs. Austin said, her voice softer.

"They need a good home." Andrew glanced at Mandy. "Particularly the mother."

Mandy stepped forward. "This is Cinders," she said, cradling the gray cat in her arms. "We think she's run wild ever since she was little. She was terrified of us to start with, and even now she's still very nervous." Mandy looked pleadingly at Mrs. Austin. "She really needs someone to love her and teach her that there's no reason to be afraid of people. She needs a good home."

Cinders opened her mouth and meowed plaintively.

Mrs. Austin's heart seemed to melt. "Poor thing," she murmured, going forward. "What a life she must have led." She looked at Mandy. "Will she let me touch her?"

"I think so," Mandy said, hoping desperately that she was right and that Cinders wouldn't panic.

"Hello, beautiful," Mrs. Austin said in a low voice, reaching out to stroke the cat.

To Mandy's relief, Cinders didn't move. She looked at Mrs. Austin with her large amber eyes and then suddenly gave a deep, rumbling purr.

Mandy took a deep breath. It looked like Cinders was going to accept Mrs. Austin. Taking a chance, she held out the little gray cat to the old lady.

A flurry of emotions crossed Mrs. Austin's face and she hesitated.

"Please, Mom," Andrew Austin said encouragingly. "You heard what Mandy said. Cinders and her kittens need a good home."

Suddenly, Mrs. Austin seemed to make up her mind.

She reached out and took Cinders from Mandy. "Poor girl," she murmured. "So you and your kittens need looking after?" She stroked the top of Cinders's head. "Well, you'll be safe and happy here with me."

"So you'll have them, Mom?" Andrew said eagerly.

Mrs. Austin smiled around at them all. "I will."

Relief flooded through Mandy. Andrew's plan had worked. At last, Cinders, Sooty, Smudge, and Sweep were going to have a real home.

"Shall I bring the kittens in for you, Mrs. Austin?" James offered.

"Yes, please," Mrs. Austin replied. "And I'll make them a bed and get some food." Cuddling Cinders in her arms, she walked into the house. James and Andrew followed.

Mandy was just about to go in, too, when she felt her mom's hand on her shoulder. "Happy now?" Dr. Emily said softly.

Mandy's eyes shone as she looked at her mom. "Very!" she said with a smile.

TM

*Read more about Mandy's animal adventures
in book #1 of the spooky new series
Animal Ark™ Hauntings*

STALLION IN THE STORM

"That must be where they stable the horses," Dr. Adam said, pointing to a large barn at the top end of the yard. Inside, two rows of about ten stalls faced each other on either side of a wide central aisle. They might have been empty, yet Mandy could hear the stamping of hooves and, now and then, a whinny from deep inside.

"Why aren't the horses looking out to see what's going on?" she asked worriedly. "It's like they're in hiding. You'd think there'd be one or two who'd want to say hello."

Dr. Adam scratched his beard thoughtfully. "Let's see if we can take a quick tour of the barn on our own," he said. "Might be interesting to see how the horses react to strangers."

They walked over to the barn, James and Mandy sticking close to Dr. Adam's side.

"I brought an apple with me," Mandy told him. "It won't stretch very far, but it might come in handy to start off with."

"Well, every little bit helps," said Dr. Adam. "Something tells me these horses aren't feeling very friendly today. They may need some persuading to come and say hello."

"Shouldn't we ask before we give them anything to eat?" asked James.

"Well, strictly speaking, we should," Dr. Adam replied, "but I don't think an apple will do too much harm. And I would like to see one or two of the horses without the stable manager looking over my shoulder."

As they entered the barn, Mandy breathed in a deep lungful of the rich straw, sweat, and leather smell that is always in the air wherever horses are kept. Then she wrinkled her nose. "I think they might need some help mucking out," she whispered to James. "It smells like it hasn't been done for a while."

"Yes, I know what you mean," he replied, just as quietly. "There's a wheelbarrow over there, but no one seems to be working today."

Dr. Adam went up to the first stall. "Come on, boy," he called to the chestnut horse inside it, who was eyeing him warily from the shadows. "We're not going to hurt you."

"Look, Dad, he's called Jupiter," said Mandy. "His name's on the door of the stall. Come here, Jupiter, and say hello."

But Jupiter wasn't going anywhere in a hurry.

"I think we may need your apple, Mandy," Dr. Adam said to her. "Do you want to have a try?"

Mandy nodded and took the apple out of her pocket. "Jupiter, look what I've got for you," she wheedled, biting off a chunk and holding it flat on her outstretched palm.

Ears lying back along his neck, Jupiter inched his way toward Mandy as she carried on talking softly. He looked ready to spring back at any moment, but her calm, quiet tone gradually seemed to be winning him over. He blew down his nose, tickling Mandy's hand, then twitched his soft, whiskery lips and daintily took the piece of apple. As he crunched, his ears flicked forward in a more friendly way, but he still eyed them warily.

"That's better," said Dr. Adam, rubbing the horse's satiny neck. "I didn't like the look of those ears, laid right back like that. But he's a nice old fellow. Aren't you, Jupiter?" He carried on chatting calmly to the horse, looking him over as far as he could.

"*Is* he old?" said James, risking a quick pat himself.

"No, he's a youngster," Dr. Adam replied. "I'd say he's probably no more than about two or three. Let's have a look at his mouth. Yes, see — he's got a couple of milk teeth still. The others are pretty straight, and not worn down at all."

"He's beautiful, isn't he?" said James, looking at the horse's dark, intelligent eyes and glossy brown coat. "He certainly is nervous, though. I wonder why?"

"I don't know," Dr. Adam replied. "But I want to find out." He turned away and began to walk down the wide central aisle of the barn, toward a dull thudding noise that had started up near the back, echoing over and over again.

"What on earth's that?" Mandy called to her father.

"One of the horses is kicking its stable door," he replied. "They develop these habits if they're bored, shut up too long in the same place."

Mandy sighed and looked deep into Jupiter's dark eyes. "What's the matter here, boy?" she asked him. "What's making you all miserable?" But Jupiter just blew down his nose at her and turned his head away, retreating to the back of the stall again.

And then, suddenly, the quiet atmosphere exploded

in noisy confusion. A clatter of hooves rang through the air outside the barn while, inside, the horses began to neigh and squeal. They wheeled around, all of them now kicking out against the sides of their stalls.

"What's happening?" cried James in alarm.

"Come on, let's go and see!" Mandy replied, rushing out toward the yard with James close on her heels. She blinked her eyes in the sudden glare of daylight — then froze in horror.

A riderless horse was heading straight for her, galloping blindly toward the entrance of the barn. It was fully saddled and bridled, stirrup irons flapping wildly against sweaty, foaming flanks. Panic showed in its rolling eyes and snorting nostrils, and the thundering clatter of its pounding hooves filled the whole yard.

"Mandy, look out!" she heard her father cry from behind her.

"Get back, Mandy!" James shouted.

But there was no time to run. Mandy crouched down against the barn wall, her arms over her head to try to protect herself. Time seemed to stand still as she waited for the impact she felt certain would follow. . . .